Ubulembu

and Other Stories

by

J. Eric Smith

Published by Unleash Press

unleashcreatives.net/press

Printed in the United States of America

ISBN 979-89-86274393

For Marcia, who believed from the beginning, with love.

TABLE OF CONTENTS

UBULEMBU

When Vigdis Thórarinsdóttir left her home in Iceland to study at Scotland's University of Dundee, she carried a small, living chunk of *Cetraria islandica* with her, wrapped in tissue and cellophane, buried deep within her suitcase. Despite its common name — "Iceland moss" — the organism was actually a hardy lichen. Her grandmother had taught her how to use its plentiful, grayish-white branches in a variety of folk medicines and traditional dishes, and its bitter taste and cartilaginous texture always evoked fond memories of her childhood. It didn't taste good, exactly, but it tasted like home, and it seemed a simple way to carry a meaningful piece of her history with her.

Vigdis was pleased to discover that her *C. islandica* clipping grew just as readily in a pot on her porch in Dundee as it had in Akureyri, and she was surrounded by several healthy clusters of the lichen when Andikan Kerk proposed to her three years after her arrival in Scotland. Andi was a South African student, and after he and Vigdis finished their studies two years later still, they were married in Dundee and set sail for his home in Sterkspruit, Eastern Cape Province, near the southwestern corner of Lesotho.

Vigdis brought sprigs of Iceland moss with her to South Africa, and once again, she was delighted to discover that it thrived in their garden along the Sterkspruit River. She and Andikan had three children, eight grandchildren, and four great-grandchildren when they died within a week of each other, at the ages of eighty-eight and eighty-nine. The world's media outlets all prominently noted their passing, and people from around the globe paused to thank them for the great gift of *ubulembu.*

ଔଔଔଔଔ

Human beings have an innate and persistent desire to achieve altered states of awareness. As a species, since time immemorial and immeasurable, we have sucked roots, nibbled stems, distilled alcoholic beverages, assumed strenuous postures, fasted, binged, smoked leaves, worshipped gods, eaten poisons, burnt oils, licked toads, sniffed chemicals, manufactured pharmaceuticals, self-flagellated, self-indulged, meditated, medicated, and investigated a seemingly endless array of methods of achieving elusive moments of otherness and difference. Sometimes we achieve it. Sometimes we don't.

Unfortunately, every successful method of achieving transcendence, however briefly, has always come with an equal (if not greater), opposite impact on us as individuals and as a species. We become addicts. We overdose. We get hangovers. We turn religious conviction into warfare against those who don't share our beliefs. We steal to finance our desires for subsequent bouts of transcendence. We rape. We are raped. We impair ourselves. We break laws and are incarcerated. We damage our minds in ways that never allow returns to normalcy. We are sad when we are no longer transcendent. We are lonely and disappointed by the world we return to. We crash. And whatever insights we may have gained from our altered states do nothing to keep us from being hungry, cold, sick, or poor.

Until *ubulembu*, that is. We now have a plentiful, cheap, easily consumed, healthy, sustainable substance that provides approximately three hours of active transcendence and weeks of afterglow, with no negative effects whatsoever. *Ubulembu* provides everyone who partakes of it with a sense of clarity and well-being, along with an abiding awakening to the utter, miraculous wonder of being a living thing, a lingering desire to share such feelings with others, and a passion for acting in ways that preserve life in all its myriad manifestations, macro and micro, known and not, seen and unseen.

Ubulembu provokes a sense of profound connection and unity and an awareness that we are not alone, as individuals, as a species, as a world. Some see what we once knew as "God" in the universal and omnipresent sense of connection that *ubulembu* provides. Others see a surety that we are not alone in the cosmos but are partners in a spectrum of life populating other planets as improbably miraculous and wondrous as our own and just as worthy of preservation.

That sense of wonder radically changed the face of the earth within two decades of *ubulembu*'s emergence, as wars of religion and misallocated resources ended, production of planet-killing instruments ceased, and the creative energies formerly dedicated to destruction were radically redirected toward ensuring the sanctity and preservation of life and the dignity and health of each individual member of the only species capable of purposeful, planet-wide action. While nations still exist today, they are little more than addresses, defining the places we live and from whence we roam, rather than borders between battling states, walls segregating resources, or barriers to common understanding and mutual affection.

By providing transcendence without some form of punishment as a direct and linked consequence, *ubulembu* finally unlocked humanity's collective creative powers, freeing us from the yokes of possessiveness and division and debasement. It is the greatest gift ever bestowed upon the planet, possibly since the first self-reproducing, interplanetary spores alighted here billions of years ago, making their home in the primordial soup of the earliest ancient seas.

ଔଔଔଔଔ

Vigdis Thórarinsdóttir Kerk didn't notice the change to her Iceland moss right away. It seemed to be growing faster than usual, and its coloration became yellower than it had been in Iceland or Scotland, but she just attributed that to different minerals in the soil or the South African climate. She was pleased to note, however, that *C. islandica* was self-propagating more readily and widely than it had before, as it began to pop up unexpectedly around her garden, then down the ravine toward the river. She wouldn't run out of it, that was for sure.

One Saturday morning in June, after a particularly hard and discouraging week of work at the Empilisweni District Hospital (where she was an administrator), Vigdis found herself cooped up inside with two restless children, trapped by a pressing rain. Seeking to brighten her mood and entertain her young ones, she decided to make a traditional porridge of her home country, using the Iceland moss, and pass that culinary cultural skill on to another generation. Two hours later, she and her children became the first human beings to experience the wonder of *ubulembu*.

When Andikan returned home that evening from his own weekend shift at the District Hospital (where he was a nurse), his wife and children rushed to embrace him and tell them of the remarkable experience they'd shared. They eagerly offered him a bowl of the porridge and sat transfixed as they watched another person experience the clarity and joy that they had shared earlier in the day. They did not feel that they had to join him. The afterglow of their own experience was sufficient, and they were not driven by any pressing need to repeat it right away.

The next day, Andi and Vigdis shared some of their porridge with one of their Xhosa neighbors. He in turn told others about the miraculous moss — *ubulembu*, in his language — that his friends had shared with him. Others soon discovered that no preparation was necessary to enjoy the benefits of the lichen: simply pulling a chunk from a plant, chewing and swallowing was sufficient to achieve the desired effect.

Within six months, the Empilisweni District Hospital was the finest in all of sub-Saharan Africa, a community choir of a thousand voices sang daily in the city square at noon, three new museums had opened in surrounding communities, six hundred new homes had been built for migrant workers, and the border with Lesotho had essentially become porous, people crossing freely in pursuit of their various enlightened activities.

By the time the international media began to take note of the growing wave of extraordinary behavior radiating outward from the Eastern Cape Province of South Africa, Andikan had sent samples of Vigdis's moss to a botanist at Rhodes University, encouraging him first to sample it personally, then to try to identify what had turned a humble lichen into such a remarkable, transformative substance. Likely fueled by the clarity that *ubulembu* provided, the botanist and his soon equally enlightened colleagues deduced the nature of the miracle.

To wit: Lichens are symbiotic organisms in which algae or cyanobacteria live among filaments of structural fungi. Vigdis's *Cetraria islandica* was uniquely predisposed to bond with a particular species of cyanobacteria in the Pseudanabaenaceae family that was resident in and around the Sterkspruit River but apparently unknown in the Northern Hemisphere, where Iceland moss had evolved. The blue-green algae's rapid acclimatization to and explosive reproduction within its new host produced a mutant species of the lichen in nearly real time, now known (obviously enough) as *Cetraria ubulembu*.

In addition to the changes in coloration and quickening in propagation (equally fecund in both asexual and sexual modes) that Vigdis had originally observed, the modified organism produced a complex organic chemical that uniquely stimulated human brain physiology, creating the effects that had theretofore evaded millennia of psychic and religious exploration. It also made the lichen far hardier: *Cetraria ubulembu* could easily be grown anyplace where humans can survive. Within a decade of its emergence, any human in the world could obtain it at will, and even the appearance of the planet from space changed, owing to its ubiquity and fecundity, its distinctive yellow-gray hue visible in satellite images of the peaceful planet it created.

Someone else might have introduced *Cetraria islandica* to the transformative Pseudanabaenaceae cyanobacteria eventually, but the world knows that it was Vigdis Thórarinsdóttir Kerk who actually did so, and she may be the most famous person in all recorded history as a result of that fortuitous geographical cross-pollination.

ଓଓଓଓଓ

The aquatic form of *Cetraria ubulembu* emerged a year or so after the gigantic motile form had pushed the last humans from Europe and Africa, and the Mediterranean Sea was filled by the end of the decade. The Bering Moss Bridge and Great Icelandic Patch closed access to the Arctic soon afterward, and both have continued pushing southward across their respective oceans since then. The Hawaiian Islands now stand as lonely mountains embedded within the southern reaches of the Pacific Moss, and the Atlantic and Mediterranean Mosses are expected to merge with the European Moss Mass within the year.

Human population has been relatively stable since the great crash of AU 180, when the global hive mind concluded inarguably that the population of humanity at that time was a net burden to the planet, ceased reproduction, and embarked upon waves of joyous community suicides. The American Commune is now home to about 250,000 souls, and the Asian Commune hosts about twice that number on interlocking networks of floating cities that ply the dwindling open seas between the moss mats.

Our collective levels of artistic, scientific, and cultural attainment are unrivaled in human history. The daily performances by the All-Commune Choirs and Orchestras can be heard by our monitoring buoys hundreds of miles away across the sea. The last hospitals closed decades ago, and our health and dietary needs are all met by the ever-expanding and mutating strains of *ubulembu*.

Our collective happiness and sense of purpose is also unparalleled in human history. Within a generation, we will leave behind a pristine planet for the *Cetraria ubulembu* to propagate upon so that it may finally reach its full reproductive maturity, flowering and launching the interstellar spores of creation spaceward, to bring other dead worlds to life, forever and ever, all across the cosmos.

We are the first, last, and only human beings to ever truly understand our purpose and place within the universe. What a gift! What an age! What happiness!

BLACKTHORN

The television service and electrical power went out at the same time, a few hours after sunset, but since everyone then living at the camp was illegally jacked into the same dish and transformer at the Engineers' Station, we didn't think much about it at the time.

Blackthorn Lake was hard-wired to civilization by only a lonely line of power poles, planted along the forty-eight-mile dirt road between here and the tiny village of Tuyona, which had a proper substation. The poles blew over or got knocked over or just fell over on their own every now and again, snapping the wires. We were used to that. There was an emergency power generator at the Engineers' Station. No worries.

That first night, folks grabbed their flashlights or lanterns, moseyed out of their dark trailers and tents, and drifted toward the little square at the center of the camp where the General Store used to be, to stretch and yawn and shuffle and see if anyone had any news. A few of us started punching at our cell phones to see if we might learn anything there, but those signals had disappeared as well. Reg said his radio was only picking up static on both AM and FM bands. So that made us wonder a bit more, but not too much. We were a long way away from everything here, even radio waves.

Ronaldo and Ivan headed over to the Engineers' Station to gas up the generator and see if they could get some juice flowing to the camp. After a few false starts, the monstrous old machine roared to life, and feeble, flickering lights appeared again around the camp. The folks who had televisions in their campers saw the screens come back on, but there weren't any pictures or sounds coming out of them, meaning either the dish was damaged by the power surge, or it wasn't receiving any signals for some other reason. Still, no biggie for anyone. It was about bedtime anyway for those who slept, and those who didn't could drink in the dark.

Morning came, and nothing had changed. Folks puttered about as they do, or they just sat and watched the world go by, which at Blackthorn Lake meant staring into the distance while nothing happened. It wasn't until late afternoon that Big Johnson started walking around to people's campsites saying, "I don't think I've heard or seen any planes overhead today. Has anybody else?"

No one had.

ଔଔଔଔଔ

I was in the laundromat in Tuyona once, and I heard somebody call the village "the ass end of the earth." If that was a true statement, then Blackthorn Lake is like the little piece of filthy toilet paper hanging off the end of a forty-eight-mile-long, gravelly hemorrhoid.

The only reason the place exists at all is because some potato farmer from up north had the crazy idea in the 1920s that he could dam the flow of the Blackthorn River at the point where it cut a steep channel between two sandstone bluffs and divert the water to irrigate the unclaimed desert land around it for spuds, the way they do in Idaho. It didn't work: the water filled in and made a shallow lake, sure, but it's so hot and so dry and so flat here that he couldn't get enough head or flow on the outbound canals to offset the effects of evaporation and soil absorption before it got to his fantasy farmlands.

In the 1930s, the Feds sent crews out on work project assignments to enlarge the lake, increase the outbound flow, and improve the dam for hydroelectric power purposes. The original lines along the access road weren't to bring power to Blackthorn Lake but to take it from here to Tuyona and beyond. And to give people jobs. The Feds built the Engineers' Station then, like a bizarre gingerbread house with fancy woodwork all around. The hydroelectric part of the project didn't work out, either, and the copper windings of the dynamos have long since been scavenged for scrap, leaving open casings sitting atop each side of the dam.

Those power improvements did make the lake a little bigger and a little deeper, though, and maybe just barely pretty enough that some people must have developed some pleasant memories of it, thinking the place could be profitably developed, somehow, by someone.

In the 1960s, the state stocked the lake with fish and tried to turn it into a sportsman's destination. That didn't work either: the fish died, and towing a boat out here was a nightmare on the undeveloped road. The 1970s saw an effort to make it more of a tourist destination as a family-friendly campsite: trails were blazed through the scrubby sagebrush around the lake's perimeter; campsites were developed for tents and trailers; a little seasonal general store was opened at the camp's center. None of that worked, either.

By the time I got here in the 1990s, the camp had become an "extended stay" site for the sorts of drifters, scoundrels, nut jobs, and loners who are drawn to the most remote sites imaginable, usually because they're running from something, or hiding from someone, or so damaged inside that they needed as little exposure to other human beings as they could possibly find. There was a little box in the booth at the camp's entrance where people were supposed to register and deposit their daily site fees when I first got here. Enforcement was feeble, at best, and eventually people stopped paying, and nobody complained.

Some folks only stayed here a little while, and some came and never left. People generally didn't say goodbye when they headed out, and they didn't generally say hello when they came back. They just appeared, or disappeared, sometimes on their own, sometimes as whole families, with children and grannies and whatnot. Folks didn't come here to socialize, so other than getting to know people's names (most of the time) and occasionally chitchat about the weather (hot, dry) or arrange a run to Tuyona, there wasn't a lot of conversation. People left each other alone and didn't ask questions. If you heard screams or cries in the night, well, that wasn't any of your business, now, was it? We all have our demons. Some of us live with them.

I'm a regular here, but not quite a permanent year-rounder; I have to go east each fall for harvest season, and I bust my ass for a month or so and scrape together enough money to tide me over, frugally, until planting season in the spring, when I leave and return again, and then the cycle repeats. I leave my beat-up trailer in my favorite spot, though, and it's been sitting there long enough that folks know not to crowd my site. I can pack everything I need for earning season in the back seat of my car, so even if someone did bust into the place, there'd be nothing for them to steal or use. Not like in the house I left behind all those years ago, with a wife and three kids and all the things they wanted, none of which they needed.

When I first got here, there were usually two Engineers here most of the time making sure the camp and the dam were monitored and the property protected, with one of them tending to the general store as well. There wasn't really much of anything for them to do (that's why they put in the television dish), but they were getting paid for it, so why would they rock that boat? Then they closed the general store one fall, and it never reopened in the spring. And then there was only one Engineer for a while, and then eventually it got to a point where someone from the Corps just came out every other week or so for a few days, checked up on things, then went back home, wherever that was.

That's when we started jacking into the station's power and television signals from their dish to improve on the "primitive" nature of the camp (that's what the old brochures on the general store bulletin board called it), and since none of the Engineers ever complained about the growing network of orange and green extension cables snaking throughout the camp, we never stopped doing it. At some point, someone jimmied the door of the general store and helped themselves to the dusty old canned goods and other supplies left behind, and that was the end of that. Once it got to that point, when folks went to Tuyona or beyond, they often took cash and requests for the whole camp. Most of the time they came back, but not always. Riffraff, remember?

So that's the history, as best I know it, for the record. There were twenty-three people living here when whatever happened, happened. There are far fewer now.

ദദദദദ

So the power went out, and the cable went out, and the phones didn't work, and the planes stopped flying over. We figured that the current Engineer would fill us in when he showed up next, but he never came. Wormy Rocky and Vince volunteered to make a run into Tuyona to figure out what was going on, and some folks gave them shopping lists and money, and off they drove. They never came back. Espo and Eva and their two kids went next. They didn't say anything to anyone, just drove off. They never came back either. I watched Sneed and Tyler go, one by one, each on his own, a day apart. Their trailing dust clouds on the dirt road were the last I saw of either of them.

I was the next one to go, sort of. I packed up my car early one morning and headed out of the camp. The land is so flat here that you can see a long way ahead of you and a long way behind. A few miles after Blackthorn Lake and the camp had disappeared behind me, I noticed something miles ahead on the road in front of me. I slowed down a bit to suss out the scene. Whatever it was, it didn't appear to be moving, so I crept up the road in low gear until I was about a quarter-mile away, got out of my car, shielded my eyes against the sun, and squinted to get a better look.

It was Sneed's pickup truck, smack in the middle of the road. Just sitting there, driver's door open, no sign of

Sneed. I reached into my car, rummaged about in the back seat and pulled out my binoculars. Scanning up ahead of Sneed's car, I saw several other bumps in the road well out in front of it. I had no doubt that I was looking at the other would-be escapees' cars, gathering dust. I didn't know what happened to their drivers, and I didn't want to. I got back in my own beater and drove back to Blackthorn.

Nobody asked where I'd gone or what I'd seen. And so I didn't tell them, because if I was stuck at Blackthorn for the foreseeable future, then the more folks who vanished elsewhere, the better off I'd be. There wasn't much to go around out here, after all.

I started writing these notes down that same night, too, so when this is over, or if someone finds us all dead out here many years from now, it might explain what we saw and help someone figure out what went down.

I was scribbling in my notebook with a candle on my table a night or two later when the first big earthquake hit. They're more common now.

ଔଔଔଔଔ

The Old Swede left, Roscoe Ruffin and his woman left, Darius Smoaks left, and the Sergeant left. And they didn't come back. And then things settled down and stabilized for the next stage, because people hunker down and adapt, you know? Especially when things are getting ready to get ugly.

There were ten of us left when people finally stopped trying to get away from here: me, Ivan, Ronaldo, Big Johnson,

Reg and his scrawny sister Regina, Tia Dona, Mad Maggie and her boy (about thirteen years old, I'd guess), and Albert the Fish. I suspect all of them had done what I had done: headed out, seen the abandoned cars, turned back, didn't talk about it. At some point, Big Johnson went around the whole camp and cajoled all of us to meet together by the general store to talk things out. It was the first (and last) time we all gathered that way. We weren't the joining or congregating type.

We had long since exhausted the gasoline left behind by the Engineers, so the generator was silent. Ivan asked if any of us were still planning to drive off, and when none of us said yes, he suggested that we siphon our vehicles and pool the available gas so that we could have power every now and then when we needed it, if for no other reason than to make sure that the television signals were still gone. Folks agreed, though I will admit that I pinched off the siphon before my gas tank was empty, just in case. I'm sure the others did, too.

Ivan and Ronaldo moved out of their trailers and into the Engineers' Station a couple of days later. The generator never came back on, and we woke one morning soon afterward to find all the power cables around the camp cut into tiny pieces. Big Johnson got drunk that night and raged at Ivan and Ronaldo outside the Station until a single gunshot fired over his head silenced him. He slunk back to his trailer, from which the sound of a second gunshot emerged a little while later. He never came out. We never went in.

I'm not quite sure exactly when or how it happened, but at some point Mad Maggie and Regina both moved into the Engineers' Station, clearly recognizing the emerging power structure of the camp. Maggie didn't take her boy with her. Tia Dona took him into her trailer, though she was sick and frail by that point, so I'm not sure what good she thought she could do for him. Maggie's boy was big and strong enough to fend for himself. He seemed to me to be tall for his age, whatever that might have been, and I'd seen him shoot more than one scrawny jackrabbit or mangy coyote with a compound bow Big Johnson had let him borrow, and he knew how to gut and field dress most of what he caught or killed. But maybe he wasn't yet so damaged for loneliness to have become a long-forgotten emotion, and maybe the little boy in him just appreciated old Tia's comfort and company. Who knows? I guess it doesn't matter, really.

Did I write about the earthquakes already? Yes, I did. Sorry, it's harder to keep track now without flipping back through this grimy notebook. Anyway, it was a major one of those earthquakes that ended this phase of the story: The camp shook hard and bounced our trailers about one afternoon, and then I heard a big boom coming from the direction of the Engineers' Station. When the ground settled, I peeked over that way out a long-since shattered trailer window, and I saw that the roof of the station had collapsed in the quake, and the walls had stove in around it.

I headed over to see what I could do, but Reg had beat me there. He was poking about in the rubble at the back of the station, and I saw him frantically digging something out of the debris. It was a red gasoline can. He pulled the top funnel off, splashed out the contents, struck a match and set fire to what remained of the station. And he laughed and jerked about like a palsy victim as the people — or the bodies — burnt up inside it. His sister included. I just watched. No one came out. No one went in.

And then there were five.

ᏣᏣᏣᏣᏣ

A few earthquakes later, the dam itself finally failed, and Blackthorn Lake drained sluggishly through the cracked earthworks, leaving a brackish, isolated pond surrounded by slimy red clay and silt. Tia Dona was gone by then, too. She just walked out to the general store square one day, lay down on her back in the sun, and died. She was the only one of us who had demonstrated any charity since whatever happened, happened, so I formulated a half-baked idea to maybe make a coffin for her, just to occupy my mind, and give her a proper burial. I thought about it for a couple of days, but then one morning when I got up, her body was gone.

No questions asked, since the food was gone by then, too, and with the lake destroyed, there weren't even any tiny, bony fish to catch any more. People do what they have to do. The land was desiccated and unproductive, birds and critters were rarely spotted, and we didn't even have any good barrel cacti around for water, so the ever-more-salty slime in the lake bed was all that was left to me, Reg, Albert the Fish and Maggie's boy. It could be that a coyote dragged Tia Dona away, or it could be that one of my neighbors did the deed, for whatever purposes were necessary. Could have been me, even. No questions, remember?

Albert the Fish wasn't so lucky. I'd already seen Reg's murderously unstable side when he burned the station, so it wasn't that much of a surprise to me some days later when I heard shouts and curses and screams and then silence emerging from Albert the Fish's old canvas tent, nor when Reg stumbled back out of its maw an hour later, bloodied, and clutching what looked like a leg wrapped up in a blanket.

I let Reg drag his spoils back to his trailer and then I waited until the sun went down, and then I waited for a few hours more, and then I pulled a hammer out of my tool kit, and then I went to Reg's trailer, and then I pushed through the screen door, and then Reg yelled and came at me, and then I hit him with the hammer, and then I hit him again, and then I beat him to death with the hammer, and then I beat what was left of him some more.

And then I walked back to my trailer, and then I went to sleep.

ଓଓଓଓଓ

I never saw Maggie's boy again. I assume he figured he was next, so he must have struck out on his own and left the camp. I still don't know what happens to people after they do that, but I'm pretty sure it's not good. Maybe going on foot will be different for him. Maybe things have changed out there. Maybe he'll go a different route, with different results. Maybe he took Big Johnson's old compound bow with him, and he'll be able to live off the land in ways that most of us couldn't. Maybe he'll be the lucky one. Probably not, though. Probably not at all.

I'm pretty sure Maggie's boy didn't see me as having avenged Albert the Fish's murder, or as having protected me and him from a similar fate at Reg's hands. He probably just saw me as yet another terrible adult doing yet another terrible thing to yet another terrible adult, while he watched or listened from the shadows. I suspect his life has been filled with that sort of thing. His mother wouldn't have ended up out here with him otherwise.

I suppose it's for the best. I'd hate to get to a point where I was driven to go after him the way that Reg went after Albert the Fish. I'll at least get to die on my own in peace here now, or be the final heroic survivor when the rescue party arrives at Blackthorn. One way or the other, it has to end. I'm OK with either path at this point.

ଓଓଓଓଓ

I heard the arrow before I saw it, and then I saw it before I felt it, sticking out of the left side of my stomach below my ribs, point forward, having entered from behind. And then it hurt. And then I screamed. And then I fell in the mud where I'd been shot, mucking about for food in the clay around what once was a lake, all those days, months, years (?) ago.

I had my tackle box with me, and I used a pair of pliers to break off the barbed head of the arrow (it was a good hunting model, only goes one way through), then reached around and pulled the shaft back through me, from behind. Terrible pain and terrible things spilled out of me.

I crawled and limped and stumbled back to my trailer, and I could sense someone (or something?) watching and waiting for me, like some ponderous, poisonous reptile that has bitten a great beast and infected it with slow-moving horrors, waiting for it to fall in due time.

I had nothing in the trailer but dirty rags to stanch the bleeding and try to keep my insides inside me. Eventually, I just gave up trying, and decided to sit outside, make a final entry in my notebook, and hope for a quick end to things.

The sun went down. And I swear to God that as I sit here waiting to die, I just saw all the stars go out.

FLEMING AND THE FOOD FLUFFERS

Fleming Jacoby marked his thirtieth birthday alone in a cheap north New Jersey motel room, pondering his life's balance sheet while eating week-old discount white cake with strawberry frosting and sipping from a can of gas station malt liquor. He had removed and flattened the top of the cake box and had drawn two columns on its oily interior, using an eyebrow pencil he'd found under the bathroom sink.

On the credit column, he wrote down: one master's degree in culinary arts, one marriage, one child, the experience of launching two great restaurants, six days left on the prepaid month in the motel room, about a third of a sheet cake, and eighty ounces of malt liquor. On the debit side, there was one unpaid student debt (rapidly accruing interest and penalties), one drunken fling with a sous-chef, one blackmail attempt, one blackmail payment, one breach of contract by a blackmailer, one divorce, one child custody case (lost), two great restaurants closed, four liens on his assets, eleven angry investors, twelve drummers drumming, and a partridge in a pear sauce, with haricots vert and a toasted quinoa pilaf.

Fleming pulled a long, slow draw from his malt liquor while perusing the greasy ledger before him. He thoughtfully drew squiggles through the "drummers" and "partridge" lines in the debit column, jiggled the can in his hand, and changed his malt liquor reserve from "80 ounces" to "maybe 60 ounces" in the assets column. Things were rapidly getting worse, clearly.

With a florid, wet malt burp, Fleming reached for the television remote and clicked the idiot box on, scrolling up to the only channel whose location he'd memorized: the Feed Me Network. He'd dreamed, once upon a time, of being one of the celebrity chefs featured on the wildly popular cable station, imagining himself in a sexy and sassy travelogue–cum–cooking show (there would have to be a lithe, Lucy Liu–like assistant) that would whip his fervid home audiences into gustatory paroxysms of secondhand sensory pleasure.

He had no idea who the schmuck serving sausages on the show was when he set down the remote, but it didn't matter, really, because he would sit there and watch that lumpen goon until the show ended, and would then probably watch five or six other shows after it, until the Feed Me Network's limited offerings began repeating themselves. Although he might keep watching even then. As would millions of other people, most of them far better off than Fleming was at the moment, with the resources to eat at any restaurant they wanted, shop at any grocery store that pleased them, and cook till the cows came home, medium rare.

In actuality, though, most of those people never cooked and rarely ate or drank anything more exotic than Fleming's sheet cake–and–malt liquor birthday fare. But damned if they wouldn't go out of their ways to look at pictures of food, and they would equally raptly listen to or watch people talking about preparing things they would never actually cook or taste.

And just how screwed up was that, really? The whole concept of food television was patently absurd when you sat back and thought about it, as everything that made food magical and sensual — the tastes, the textures, the smells — was neutered when watching it broadcast from afar. Fleming's restaurants had been objectively exceptional, customers and critics agreed, but he could never generate enough loyal business to keep them open for more than a couple of years, and he had come to believe that his failure was because the folks who once would have been his most loyal customers found it preferable to look at food in the dank privacy of their own homes, rather than eat it in public with others. He was not made to cook for these times, clearly.

"Food porn" was a perfect phrase for the phenomenon, Fleming thought, as it turned a beautiful experience best shared with other people into something solitary, creepy, ultimately unsatisfying — and yet strangely, wholly addictive. Fleming had never been able to get customers to feel that same hungry addiction for his exquisitely crafted restaurant offerings. And absent a television contract or an expensive website or a glossy ad campaign, there was obviously no way for him to have turned his restaurants into peepshows where people could satisfy their apparent prurient desire to watch but never taste.

And then Fleming Jacoby had his million-dollar food idea, along with his last swig of gas station malt liquor.

ଓଓଓଓଓ

The equipment was cheap and readily available, since New York had cracked down on live sex shows during the Great Disneyfication of Times Square. Owners were eager to sell at a bargain the idle two-room booths that hoovered up dollar bills in return for peeks through a viewing window between a private client seating area and a small stage area where a performance (whatever it might be) occurred. Fleming self-financed his investments by spending several months with his mother on Long Island after his motel lease ran out, stealing and selling his father's coin, rare book, and stamp collections along the way. Dad wouldn't mind, Fleming figured, what with being dead and everything. He was just taking his inheritance sooner than Mom might have liked, and she was happy to have him home and wasn't likely to notice the missing materials.

The concept was simplicity itself, the ultimate distillation and dirtying down of the food porn experience. Each booth would have a menu posted on its exterior door, laying out two to four courses of interesting dishes. Customers would pick a menu of their liking, enter the associated booth, close the door behind them, sit on the stool within, feed their bills into the machinery slot in the wall before then, and sit alone to happily ogle the prepared dishes on the other side of the glass — until the timing mechanism shut the sash on the window abruptly, hopefully sooner than the customer was really ready to stop food peeping.

Fleming didn't know why people would want to do that, but his gut told them that they would, and they would pay for the privilege, more than once. He wrote his own press materials and sent them to the various traditional and digital media outlets that traded in the sorts of quirky, experiential stories which foodies and hipsters and hipster foodies ate up and Retooted or Faceblogged or Instapinned or whatever the hell else it was that they did that allowed them to all know the same things in the same ways at the same time.

And they ate it all up, so to speak, even as they would never eat it up, literally. On opening night at Fleming's Fabulous Food Forum (as he dubbed it, modestly), the line to enter wound well around the Brooklyn block outside of the nondescript (read: cheap) storefront with roll-down security screen that Fleming had picked for his new venture. He'd cajoled two former restaurant employees to help him prepare and maintain the plates, promising them that he'd split opening week proceeds with them three ways, regardless of how things turned out, then turn them into hourly employees if there was to be a second week.

Week one played out stunningly well for the three of them, and so there was indeed a second week. And then a third one, then a fourth, then expanded hours, then extra booths leased and slotted into the congested lobby area to meet demand. Fleming hired two more "Food Fluffers" (the team all quickly dropped into the patois of porn) and created a few seven- and even nine-course premium display booths where the cash required to keep the window open for more than seconds at a time would rapidly deplete the wallets of the most desperately salivating "Long Johns" (as they'd dubbed their clients — see "patois of porn," above).

Demand was so intense that Fleming soon had to hire a phone service to preschedule blocks of time for the booths of highest interest; prescheduling was sold at double the price of drop-in time. And for the hardest of hardcore Long Johns, who were willing to double their payments once again after prescheduling their booth times, one of the Food Fluffers would stand inside the booth with the food, describing in loving detail how the dishes had been prepared, with what ingredients, at what temperatures, and with what utensils. Whisk play seemed to be particularly popular.

A month or so later, Fleming began posting menus outside the building, so that the most loyal Long Johns could check to see when things had been freshened with new seasonal ingredients, oftentimes passing the building multiple times a day in the hopes that some dirty new food thrill would be awaiting them as reward for their troubles. One of the city's most famous food critics paid a visit and wrote warmly, lovingly, and enthusiastically about the food he viewed at the Fabulous Food Forum. The story was picked up nationally, and people began to travel to New York just to visit Fleming's not-quite-a-restaurant.

Six months into the venture, Fleming Jacoby had amassed enough personal profit to move back into a small apartment in Manhattan (where he belonged), to settle debts with several of his creditors, to make a good-faith payment on his student loans, and to buy his ex-wife and still-son an assortment of expensive Christmas presents, which his mother delivered, because of the restraining order and everything. He had intentionally hired only male Food Fluffers to reduce the likelihood of bad workplace behavior that might further estrange him from his family — and he always had himself photographed with his mostly dumpy team when the media stopped by, just in case his ex was paying attention. Well, also because it made him look more handsome in comparison, just in case anybody else's exes were paying attention too.

Fleming had arrived. Again. And as the new year dawned, he again began to frequently imagine a future filled with greatness and renown and lithe, Lucy Liu–like assistants (strictly professional), just as he had when he had opened his two real restaurants.

Which, of course, is when the wheels fell off.

ଓଓଓଓଓ

With hindsight, he could and should have seen it coming. The signs and pitfalls and risks were there right from the beginning, but as long as the money was rolling in, it was easy to ignore them.

The earliest problems to arise had to do with the behavior of some of the Long Johns, as best evidenced by the ever-growing cleaning efforts and costs required to keep the booths suitable for use. Apparently, some Long Johns weren't actually happy just to look at food but instead surreptitiously brought in their own illicit snacks, consuming them in the booths behind closed doors. Fleming and the Food Fluffers began to receive regular complaints about Bavarian cream streaks, chutney spills, ketchup spatters, residue of white powdered sugar, and other annoyances being left behind in the booths, and one time Fleming found a whole steaming pile of Blutwurst on the floor, still warm, links still connected one to the other.

Then the widely known laws of addiction tolerance kicked in, dictating that what had thrilled a given Long John a month ago wouldn't push his buttons today, so to get the same desired pleasure required ever more arcane dishes and presentations. The Fluffers did yeoman's work making tall food, framing microportions, incorporating nonedible props, using Sterno to create bubbling volcanic sauce flows, plating entrees on colorful combinations of smears and drizzles and purees and demiglaces that looked like explosions in a finger paint factory and whatever else they and Fleming could come up with to keep ahead of the most demanding Long Johns' rising expectations.

But it was never enough, because at some point, a hamburger made out of cow is a hamburger made out of cow, no matter what you put on top of it, what you did with the cow before you turned it into hamburger, what machinery you used to make that conversion, and what sorts of grainy things you put it all between or smeared it with. So you had to make that burger with buffalo meat the next time to get the desired thrill and command the continued dollars. And then you had to move on to ostrich. And then to musk ox. And then to crocodile. And then to elephant.

And then to onager, which Fleming now knew to be a rare Mongolian horse, classified as "near-threatened" by the International Union for the Conservation of Nature. He hadn't been aware of that when he purchased six pounds of its shanks (bone in) from an exotic meats supplier in Little Italy. He had bought the onager meat at the specific request of one of his most insistent Long Johns, who always made his demands in writing online, always reserved his booths in advance at whatever price Fleming set for him (assuming he'd acquired the desired goods), never requested Food Fluffer narration, and always entered and exited the Forum quickly, typically in sunglasses and with a hoodie pulled up over his head.

As it turned out, the secretive Long John was an undercover agent of the United States Department of Agriculture's Animal and Plant Health Inspection Service, and the story of Fleming's succumbing to his sting operation received even more extravagant national front-page coverage than had the Fabulous Food Forum's opening and early successes.

And so Fleming Jacoby marked his thirty-first birthday alone in the Metropolitan Detention Center in Brooklyn, New York, awaiting his trial on charges that he had attempted to import animals (or at least bits of animals) protected under international law from commercial exploitation. His lawyer told him that the "attempted" part was really important, since the onager meat had actually been just a lamb shank, and so no actual crime had actually occurred (the lawyer said), even though the financial transaction between Fleming and the Italian meat man (also a USDA spook) had been predicated on the presumption that Fleming was willfully breaking the law. No hurt, but still a foul, apparently.

Fleming's mother had come to visit him a day earlier, and she spent their entire hour together explaining the new home security system she had installed when she realized that burglars had stolen her late husband's most prized and beloved collectibles. The Nassau County police were on the trail, and she was certain that justice would be served, with the nefarious perp(s) tossed behind bars to rot, hopefully sooner rather than later, so they could suffer longer for their sins.

Fleming nodded and smiled wanly as she talked, absentmindedly dreaming of lithe, Lucy Liu–like assistants all the while.

THE DIVINE OFFICE

Mère Maelle Favager and Tante Priskilla Cloutier were sent after Lauds to feed the fathers and prepare the hands for the field, duties which released them that day from their obligation to pray the Divine Office of Prime with the other sisters.

It was for this reason that they were the first to see the ship stranded on the shoals east of Îles Saint-Wivina, its luffing sails casting undulating shadows across the waters as the wan morning sun rose behind them, blanched by the ever-present haze surrounding the scruffy islets.

Knowing the crucial importance of haste in responding to such maritime emergencies in the treacherous waters surrounding Îles Saint-Wivina, Mère Maelle and Tante Priskilla immediately hiked their woolen smocks up to their knees and ran for the abbey as quickly as their felted clogs would allow, ululating as they hurried to alert the other sisters assigned non-prayerful duties for the day. Fille Yehudit Lefurgey joined them as they passed the smokehouse, and Tante Haggith Agar fell into line behind the trio soon thereafter, but only after removing the community's daily flatbreads from her oven, partially cooked wafers being preferable to burnt ones.

The other sisters were still praying Prime when the four concerned women arrived at the abbey, so the quartet lowered their heads prayerfully and waited outside the sanctuary until the final capitulum and versicle had been completed, and the conjoined voices of the other sisters finally fell silent.

"There's a ship on the shoals, Abbess Mehetabel," shouted Tante Priskilla, the oldest and most experienced of the women. "We must hasten to the harbor and send the coracles forth!"

Abbess Mehetabel Deniaud emerged from the sanctuary at the head of a line of gray-cloaked sisters, ranging in age from filles of less than five years old to tottering tantes in their nineties. She dispatched Mère Colombe Sauvageau to the fields to bring six of the hands, and then, with no further words spoken, the women marched in line with purpose toward the harbor.

While their island community was breathtakingly isolated from a mainland dweller's perspective, it was just close enough to shipping lanes in and out of the vast Rivière du Berno to occasionally waylay wayward vessels in its murky mix of sand and shoals, rocks and reefs, winds and mists, and treacherous, tide-fueled currents.

The sisters and hands of Îles Saint-Wivina had, through generations of trial and error, learned the secrets of navigating and fishing about their islands. They deployed shallow coracles and kept them lightly loaded, the better to ride the currents and avoid the many hazards below the waterline. They rarely sailed but used paddles and oars, allowing more rapid response to shifting conditions. Steering was controlled not by a fixed rudder but by using variable paddle pressures and placement, fine-tuning the forces acting on the coracles from all directions.

Travel from point A to point B across their waters was rarely linear, but often followed circuitous routes through known channels and into familiar currents. The sisters and hands timed their forays around the dramatic tides, knowing that certain routes were possible only when the tide rose, others when it fell, and attempting some only when the most extreme neaps and ebbs provided propulsive power to supplement human exertion.

Many of their techniques flew in the face of traditional deep-water sailors' training and instincts, as they'd witnessed many times over the years. Upon grounding, sailors tended to pack their boats as heavily as they could with people and provisions and beeline for the shore before their ships broke apart. Countless scores of sailors had perished this way within the memories of the current sisters, as their small boats were breached, broken, and battered, their contents either sucked below into the unforgiving mud (sailors often grabbed gold and silver coins and were drowned by their own heavy fortunes) or pulled far out into the Rivière du Berno's vast estuary, where they would circle helplessly in the cold, briny water until material or human fatigue overwhelmed them.

Their ships didn't last long after running aground at Îles Saint-Wivina, either, as they tended to beach at a point just outside a barrier shoal but atop a steep submarine escarpment. The power of the waves was at its strongest there, as they rode up the scarp, funneled like air into a nozzle, then blasted freely into the hulls at the surface, rhythmically and repeatedly pounding them at the same spots on the same sides while the tides pushed in, followed by a palpable vacuum pulling the other way as the tides rushed back out. Damaged hulls were invariably breached by the extreme forces at play far more rapidly than they would be on most shores.

It was a hellish seascape, and the sisters and hands of Îles Saint-Wivina understood that quick and direct action was required so that the beached sailors would stand fast, pleading their patience until the sisters and hands could ferry them ashore on the coracles, in the only ways that offered even moderate probability of success and survival.

The hands were much heavier than the sisters, so they pulled coracles out on their own, while the sisters paired up in theirs. Abbess Mehetabel put forth with Mère Maelle, pulling to the front of the small flotilla of thirteen coracles (crewed by six hands and fourteen sisters) as it wound its way between the harbor and the stranded ship.

Within minutes of getting under way, all the sisters and hands could see frantic activity on the decks of the ship, now visible as a deep-water fishing vessel sailing under Basque colors, undoubtedly chasing cod across the Rivière du Berno. As was typical, the sisters and hands watched the sailors lowering boats, hauling stores from below, flapping their arms against the damp cold, and minding a trio of apparent officers or merchantmen who were watching the incoming small boats to assess threats.

As the fleet of coracles approached the damaged merchant ship, Abbess Mehetabel's timepiece sounded the chime for the Office of Terce. She called across the water for Fille Yehudit and Fille Florianne Despujols (in one coracle) and Tante Priskilla and Tante Haggith (in another) to pray the office on behalf of the community, and with oars moving just enough to hold their places, those four sisters began to sing as the remaining coracles pressed on. Many of the sailors on deck removed their hats or helmets, and they crossed themselves, some confusion on their faces.

Abbess Mehetabel Deniaud hailed the crew of the ship in Latin as they drew close. After some milling about on deck, a tonsured head appeared at the rail.

"Good fray," shouted the abbess above the prayers still being sung from two slowly spinning coracles. "We are a faithful island community humbly given to Our Sweet Lord's service. These seas are treacherous and likely fatal to your men if they continue their attempts to load your longboats and make for shore. We have many years of experience in sailing these waters and shepherding similarly stranded sailors ashore, and we are here in Our Sweet Lord's name to ferry your men safely to the island. We know, too, from experience that you must no doubt perceive this as a most unusual circumstance, so we will leave two of our order here with you on your ship as proof of our good will, trusting in good faith to your own virtue, until we have safely ferried your men to solid ground."

Abbess Mehetabel gestured to the coracle nearest the ship just as the Office of Terce was completed, and Tante Ossane Pouline and Tante Heloise Comtois rowed together toward the Basque ship, bobbing below its rails. Aftcr what seemed a long period of animated conversation on the deck, a rope ladder was tossed down, and Tante Ossane and Tante Heloise climbed it, disappearing over the rail some minutes later.

"A shallow draft is essential to safe passage to shore," shouted Abbess Mehetabel. "We can ferry one sailor per coracle and make way through the channels and passages approaching the shore. How many men are aboard your vessel?"

"*Viginti quattuor*," shouted back the Friar.

"We have twelve crewed coracles here now, leaving one behind for our sisters aboard, so it will take us two trips to ferry all twenty-four of you," responded the Abbess. "Send down your first two men, and we will ferry them to shore first, so that you can confirm their safe passage and our good faith. Once they are in the harbor, then we will shuttle eleven more en masse, and return for the remainder of your men as quickly as we are able. We should be able to get all of your crew to shore before the Divine Office of Vespers, and with Our Sweet Lord's grace, your ship will survive the night so that we may return tomorrow to attempt salvage as best we may, and send a boat into the Rivière du Berno in an attempt to hail passage for you back to your homeland. You will be our welcome guests until that time."

After another long exchange on the deck, two men began to descend the rope ladder. Abbess Mehetabel smiled at the view: it was typical that ships in such straits would send those men they considered most expendable down to the first coracles, and the Basques had clearly done the same, with what appeared to be a cabin boy and a ship's cook. The two young men stepped from the ladder into a pair of coracles, each of which was crewed by one of the hands.

Without a word, the two hands began the journey back to the harbor, deftly winding their way through the flats, channels and shoals, often flowing backward atop wave crests to move forward with the subsequent stronger wave cycle, working to stay atop the lively surface currents and avoid the rip tides and shallows beneath them, closely tuned to the waters to most effectively redirect the sea's and the wind's energies for their own purposes.

It took nearly forty minutes, but the hands and their passengers finally reached the harbor, tied off, and climbed atop the ramshackle pier. The cabin boy and the cook waved back across the waters at their compatriots, and a polite but authentic cheer arose from the Basque merchant ship's deck. The other ten coracles moved into place, one by one, below the rope ladder, each accepting a single member of the crew and beginning the erratic journey back to shore.

Abbess Mehetebel and Mère Maelle's coracle was the last to pull up to the rope ladder, and recognizing their seniority, one of the officers or merchantmen began to climb down to join them, respectfully bowing to thank them for their assistance before he began his descent. They nodded their heads modestly, quietly pleased with the recognition of their service.

"We shall return as soon as we able to ferry the rest of you ashore," shouted Abbess Mehetebel. "We trust you will keep Tante Ossane and Tante Heloise safe and secure until then, and we humbly request that you might let them go below decks to get warm after a chilled morning spent on the water, even to your brig or a secure space in your hold if you'd prefer not to have to mind them as you secure your ship and prepare for transit to the harbor. They can happily busy themselves there with prayer until our return, as Tante Ossane has a timepiece to mark the hours of the Divine Office."

Before they arrived at the shore, Abbess Mehetebel's own timepiece sounded the chime for the Office of Sext, and she hailed Fille Florianne and Tante Haggith to sing the prayers from two different coracles, so that their companions could continue the push back to shore. Some of the Basques joined in quietly during the Kyrie and the Lord's Prayer, their miraculous rescue seemingly moving them to fits of observant faith.

As each coracle tied off at the pier, the sisters or hands helped the Basques from the bobbing boats and led them to shelter in the large storage warehouse at the base of the pier, entering via a low door with a vestibule in an alleyway on the north side of the building that protected the entrance from direct sunlight, rain, and wind.

In pairs, the sisters left the warehouse and returned to the pier after leaving their charges behind, gathering again as a group to watch the ship. The hands did not return to the pier from the warehouse.

Just as Abbess Mehetebel's timepiece sounded the chime for the Office of None, two explosions ripped the hull of the Basque ship. Tante Ossane and Tante Heloise had detonated the heavy gunpowder sacks they carried beneath their garments, and by the looks of the crumbling hull on the shoreward side of the ship, the Basques had taken to heart Abbess Mehetebel's request to put them below decks. A subsequent explosion indicated they'd even been placed near the magazine battery. How blessed they were by the sisters' Sweet Lord to enter glory so successfully!

Sailors could be seen on decks as the smoke cleared, then climbing into the rigging as the hull began to break apart before the retreating sea. In the best of circumstances and with all the proper knowledge and equipment, it would take them nearly an hour to get to shore, at which point they could be easily apprehended by the hands. But few ever got that far, most instead being sucked out to spin in the vast mouths of the Rivière du Berno.

Abbess Mehetebel led the sisters back into the warehouse. The twelve Basque sailors lay bound and gagged on straw in the middle of the room. Each had been struck with a truncheon by one of the hands as they stooped to enter the low, dark entryway. The hands knew just the best spot for a strike, to quickly and silently render the sailors unconscious without doing any permanent structural damage. Some still moved groggily, some were still limp, and some writhed against their bonds, sharp-eyed in rage and fear.

The Abbess raised her hands and stood above the first of the sailors. As the Divine Office divides the day into six portions, so she divided the sailors into six groups by pointing, crossing herself, and speaking a single word before raising her hands again in a supplicant's pose.

Before the cabin boy, she said "Field."

Before the cook, she said "Sea."

Before the next sailor: "Fire."

Before the gracious officer: "Father."

Before the next sailor: "Blood."

Before the next sailor: "Fire."

"Blood."

"Glory."

"Father" (this was the tonsured monk).

"Glory."

"Field."

And before the last of the Basques: "Sea."

The sisters and the hands all crossed themselves, then divided themselves into six well-organized groups. Each group roughly pulled two of the struggling sailors behind them through outward opening doors at the west end of the warehouse, away from the waterfront and the view of the sea.

The Field group dragged their sailors to the pastures, where the oldest of the hands slit each of their throats. The group then dragged the bodies around the field to allow the sailors' blood to penetrate the soil. Another hand dragged in a tiller and a plow, which would be used to turn the sailors' bones, viscera, and flesh under the soil to benefit the next year's crops.

The Sea group repeated a similar ritual at the harbor, one sailor's blood being drained into the water, one sailor's blood being dripped atop each of the coracles. Their bodies were left on the pier for the night and would then be taken the next morning beyond the deep water escarpment and consigned to the depths.

The Fire group used their sailors' blood to bless the foundry where metalwork was completed. Their bodies would be burned in the forges.

(As the groups worked through their tasks, they paused at the appointed time to pray the Holy Office of Vespers.)

Mère Maelle led the Glory group, which took their two sailors into the abbey's sanctuary and spilled their blood on the altar therein. Their bodies would be dried and ground into the mortar used to repair the sacred space.

Fille Yehudit directed the Blood group, leading the sailors, sisters, and hands to the smokehouse. These sailors' blood was spilled more carefully into jugs, so that it could be stored and used for sacramental purposes, since no wine grapes grew on Îles Saint-Wivina. The sailors' drained remains would be salted, smoked, and stored to keep them until wintertime, when fishing became impossible and protein difficult to obtain.

And Abbess Mehetebel Deniaud led the Father group. These two sailors were bestowed the greatest honor of all: the perpetuation of the order. Rather than spilling their blood, the hands used a heavy axe to deftly remove their right hands and left feet, then cauterized their wounds with heated iron plates from the foundry, finally wrapping the wounds with cloths and ointments proven to facilitate healing. The hobbled sailors were then taken to the fathers' dormitory, where eight other similarly incapacitated men resided, all well fed, all given books, paper, pens, games, and other sundries upon request, all as comfortable as island life would allow.

When the young women of the island turned twenty-one years old, each was given three months to lie with one of the fathers, selected by the abbess, as frequently (or not) as the fille wished. Those women who became heavy with child in the months that followed and bore offspring were then recognized as mères; those who did not became tantes instead.

Once a father had sired three children or failed to impregnate three filles, he would be prayerfully assigned by the abbess to the Field, Sea, Fire, Blood, or Glory path, and prayerfully dispatched in accordance with that group's mandate.

The birth of a girl child — a new fille — was always greeted with great celebration by the sisters. The child was named, raised by the mères, and educated in the ways of the order.

The birth of a boy child — while equally necessary — provoked a lesser degree of excitement. Boys were not named but instead were castrated and sent to the hands' dormitory, where they were raised by the tantes until self-sufficient enough to be cared for by the other hands and taught their duties in service of the community.

Two hundred and forty-eight years had passed thus since the founding of the order on Îles Saint-Wivina. Their Sweet Lord Abezethibou of Tartarus had blessed and kept and provided for them very well indeed, time and time again.

Amen.

HOW DO YOU KNOW?

How do you know?

Know what?

What you know.

Well, I learn things, I guess. I read. I listen. I study. I talk. I assimilate. I process. Once I learn something, then I know it. Is that what you mean?

No.

Can you tell me what you mean in a different way, then?

When I took your ship, I tried to know you in the way that knowing beings know each other, but I could not know you, and you could not know me. I found a cup on the outside of your ship, and when I knew the cup, the cup knew you. How?

You began speaking to me through my ship's communications feed. I heard you, which means you caused a membrane in a speaker to vibrate in a way that caused membranes in my head to vibrate sympathetically, and the signals those membranes created were transmitted to my brain, so in hearing you, I learned you were there, or I knew you were there. I use another organ in my head to create other vibrations that move other membranes in other speakers, which apparently you can understand via the communications dish on the outside of my ship. The dish, or the cup you know, is a communications link that broadcasts these vibrations to my home world. So I know you are here, and I can hear you, and speak to you, but I do not know who or what you are. I know that you are directing my ship and that I cannot override your direction. I know that you have taken my ship away from the ships of my companions, and that I cannot communicate with them. I assume that this is because you have overridden my communications dish, and are using it to navigate my ship, communicate with me, and perhaps communicate with others of your kind?

I do not have a membrane. I do not vibrate. I know. But you know me without me knowing you, and I do not know how you know.

I suppose, yes. I would say that I know of you, but I do not know you. Who are you?

I am the one who knows me most knowingly.

Are there others like you?

There are ones who know themselves most knowingly, and know others.

Are you a machine, or are you a living being?

I am a knowing being.

Well, yes, I understand that, I think, but are you a living being, or something else, like a thinking machine, a device that can know? This ship is a machine. The communications dish you are using to speak with me and guide the ship is a machine. But a machine is not alive. I am alive, a living being. Organic. Birthed by other living beings, not made.

I know the cup on the ship. The cup knows you. I cannot know you. I am a knowing being.

OK, but were you manufactured, or were you born?

I became.

I don't know, then. I cannot see you, only hear you, so I don't know if you are a machine or a living being. I suppose it doesn't matter. Why have you taken my ship?

It is why I became.

You came into being to take my ship? Or ships in general? Are you a pirate? An explorer? A scientist? Why do you want to take my ship in a direction different from the one that it was traveling in with the others of my kind? The direction that I and my people picked. That we know, I suppose, as you would say.

I know many ships. I know many knowing beings who know ships. It is why I became. I know your ship through its cup, but I cannot know you. I have never known a ship that did not contain a knowing being that I could know.

My fellows and I are the first of our people to travel to this star system. We are on a journey of colonization in advance of the likely destruction of our world through environmental disasters made by our own kind. We have never been this far from our home sun. We have never known other living beings that have shown the intelligence you have shared with me. I feared my ship had malfunctioned when it suddenly went off course and I was unable to communicate with my fellows. But apparently that is when you began to know my ship, and your intelligence, your knowing, is apparently greater than ours. Or at least very, very different. And powerful.

I cannot know you. You are a nonknowing being. Nonknowing beings are not normally found alone on ships. They are normally transported only to feed knowing beings that have yet to shed their husks.

You do not have a husk?

I could not know your ship in open space if I had a husk.

Do you feed, then?

Yes.

On what?

Ships.

And what do you normally do with the knowing beings inside the ships?

Know them.

I don't understand. What happens to them after you know them, but before you feed on their ships?

I know them. Then they know me. Then we become.

Become what?

Me.

And you cannot know me?

I cannot know you.

And you are going to feed on my ship?

I am going to feed on your ship.

So you are going to feed on me as well, then?

I feed on ships.

Then what is going to happen to me?

I cannot know.

Can I know?

No.

BLACKBERRIES

Rosamunde stood in her kitchen drinking cold blackberry tea and surveying the stout hedges, knotted and overgrown, that defined her short horizon in every direction.

Some mornings, she could discern visible changes over the prior twenty-four-hour period, as the piles of brambles responded to favorable rain and sun conditions, their already impressive growth rate opportunistically accelerating even further, lest the days to come be less favorable for them. But it had been hazy and cold yesterday, so the hedges seemed quiescent for the moment, their menace potential, not kinetic, their distance from her house and shed still just beyond the circle of stones Rosamunde and her father had placed around their haven a few years earlier.

She wouldn't have to prune today, thankfully, so she could finally tend to the other matter that had been weighing on her mind for the prior week. She knew she had a hard day's work ahead of her, so before heading out to the shed, she slowly chewed three dried earthworms, savoring their salty, protein-rich earthiness as a welcome contrast to the cloying sweetness of the inescapable blackberries.

She had loaded the box atop her ramshackle wagon, strapped and balanced as closely to the center of gravity as she could get it, in hopes of being able to drag it along the few narrow pathways through the hedges that remained. She and her father had worked on the box together, scavenging boards from unused cabinets and floors in empty rooms, binding them with young blackberry shoots and spare bits of wire and metal that they could scavenge from around the haven. It was rickety, but it would do the job.

Rosamunde's father had weighed less than eighty pounds when he died, so it was not difficult for her to place him in the box, carefully folding his limbs to fit inside before rigor mortis set in. She was grateful that she had been present when he passed, as she had long had nightmares of having to use her pruning equipment on her father's body to get his remains into a tiny coffin or other such container.

Which was her necessity, and his choice. Her father's last flint had long since worn too smooth to strike a spark, so barring a fortuitous lightning bolt, Rosamunde had no way to cremate him when his old body finally wore out. And he had wanted to be buried, anyway, old beliefs and convictions still strong in a new world where they had neither anchor nor relevance, except as warm reminders of that which once was.

Rosamunde's father had picked out a spot between the house and the shed where he wanted to be buried, and Rosamunde had humored him about its desirability, knowing that this was the one request of his that she wasn't going to honor. Her recurring nightmares of having to cut her father into pieces often ended with her turning him into steaks, or jerky, or cakes, or something, anything, food-related beyond blackberries and worms, the only sources of nutrition they'd been able to procure consistently over the past . . . well, however long it had been, she actually didn't know anymore.

Knowing firsthand the extents to which hunger could press a person, Rosamunde was unwilling to have her father's remains buried anywhere she could ever get at them should her situation ever lead her to such an insane act of desperation.

She had quietly decided months ago to consign him to the blackberries, following a path deep into the brambles, clearing a spot in some isolated corner, burying him at the foot of one towering vine or another, knowing that she would never be able to make her way back to his final resting spot, as it would inevitably be covered and buried beneath the bulk of the inexorable hedges.

When she was younger, there had been more paths around the island, some occasionally even allowing Rosamunde and her father to access the sea, where they collected shellfish and the eggs of shorebirds. But the blackberries were now thickest and strongest along the perimeter of the island, and it had been many years since they'd been able to hack their way through the dense walls of knotted wood along the shores. This always reminded them why pruning along their haven's perimeter was so important: they didn't have the strength to cut through anything thicker than half an inch or so, and the blades of their remaining tools were getting alarmingly thin and dull as they had sharpened them on stones over the years.

Animals had blazed some of the earlier trails through the living maze, as they had since time unmemorable, before the radical transformation of the landscape that destroyed their habitats. The last mammal Rosamunde had seen was a bedraggled, mangy fox, snooping around the border of their haven, desperate for scraps, some months back. She had felt sorry for the forlorn beast, but not so much that she didn't try to catch and kill it for meat, getting her final glimpse of the frightened fox as it disappeared back into the brambles with a sad bark of dismay.

These days, the blackberries themselves seemed to create the paths between them, though there was neither rhyme nor reason to their routes. Sometimes the understories of the plants would die down, creating tunnels beneath the sun-baked canopy. Sometimes rocks or otherwise unattractive soil conditions would create lasting breaks between the twisted trunks and stems, leaving passable gaps. And sometimes storms would knock large stands over, crushing their neighbors and creating temporary, passable breaks before the next generations of blackberries propagated.

There was a fairly stable, rocky-bedded path out of the haven on its sunset side, and Rosamunde occasionally walked into the brambles along it to assess the state of things beyond her little circle of security, ever hopeful that perhaps some new breach had occurred, for some sign of die-back that might indicate that the blackberries' reign had run its course. But that never happened, and the network of subsequent paths into the brambles at the end of that rocky tongue seemed different every time she reached it.

Today, she resolved to follow the sunset-side trail farther away from the haven than she had been in quite some time. She had loaded a collection of shiny, metal objects from her kitchen and bedroom onto the wagon bearing her father's remains and would use them to mark intersections, if necessary, to guide her back home, hopeful that their sheen would make them easy to identify in the rapidly changing landscape of green leaves, brown stems, and black globules of fruit.

The wagon moved surprisingly easily once she put her back into pulling it and got it rolling, and she reached the end of the rocky spit into the brambles fairly quickly. She paused there to look back, seeing only a corner of her house still, beneath the overarching branches of the berries. The air was cool and damp inside the hedges, and her stillness of the undergrowth amplified her breathing, made it sound like something outside herself.

There were two larger tunnels into the undergrowth to her right and a smaller one to her left, the latter looking like it might have been opened by a section of the canopy having fallen over. Knowing that her mission was to place her father someplace where she couldn't reach him again, she chose the smaller, less obvious and less sustainable path.

Before she entered its mouth, she shoved a spoon into a crack in the underlying stone, pointing back toward the haven. Just in case.

Rosamunde could only advance into the breach slowly and with difficulty for a few hundred feet beneath the canopy, at which point the path veered sharply to the left, widened, and unexpectedly opened to the sky above her. She stretched her back and shook out her cramped legs and arms.

Before continuing, Rosamunde placed a doll's silver teapot at the turn in the trail, its spout pointed homeward.

The wall to her right now was particularly gnarled and knotted, much like the coastal perimeter that the blackberries had established on the island. Its density appeared to have curtailed growth on what she presumed was its landward side, so she had easier going for the next segment of her journey, which ended when she came upon a large, flat stone, atop which no brambles grew, affording another clear view of the sky above her.

A tiny break in the hedges was visible off to the left, but it appeared to reach either a dead end or a turn at the farthest reach of Rosamunde's vision. As it was the only path out of the clearing besides the one she'd entered by, she decided to continue, but only after laying down a gaudy chrome slide whistle on the flat stone, its mouthpiece pointing back toward the teapot and the spoon and the haven.

She grunted and strained as she pushed and pulled her wagon and its load into the gap between the hedges. As she'd expected, the fissure finally became impassible some fifty feet in, but the soil at that point was reasonably soft and sandy, and Rosamunde figured that it would be overgrown again in no time at all, so she decided that her father had reached the end of his road. She shoved his box off the wagon and onto the ground at the base of the brambles, removed her small spade from the wagon, and dug as quickly and deeply as she could with it, working up a clammy sweat in the dark, moist crevice within the island's living armor.

After about an hour of toil, Rosamunde had created a hole that was roughly three-quarters as deep as her father's box was tall, and she figured that was good enough, under the circumstances. She dragged the box into place and used her spade to stack up the soil she'd removed from the hole around and atop it, as best she could. She then scavenged about the tiny hollow for rocks, placing them atop the box. Finally, she looked for young tendrils within the surrounding vines and pulled them down, lacing them around the box's imperfections, hoping they would grasp and grow into it, facilitating the return of its contents to the sandy loam beneath it.

As she began to back out of the verdant crevasse, she continued to pull vines and tendrils and branches across the trail, hoping to speed the closure of the gap and thereby putting her mind at ease that her father would rest unmolested deep within the heart of the hedges, no matter what happened in the days or months or years to come. At some point, though, specific worries about being trapped in the brambles now began to supersede vague worries about what might happen tomorrow, so Rosamunde eventually turned her back on her father's grave and pulled her wagon forward toward the stone opening, as quickly as she could pull it.

As she cleared the brambles, she was relieved to see a glint of metal in the middle of the flat stone, reflecting the sun above it. She rolled her wagon up to the stone, stood and stretched her back, raised her arms above her head, let the sun warm her face, and tried to remember an appropriate prayer for such a day.

Failing to do so after a few seconds of halfhearted effort, Rosamunde shrugged, then walked forward to retrieve the chrome slide whistle that would direct her to her next waypoint.

Except that she found the doll's silver teapot sitting there instead, its spout unequivocally pointing toward the solid, impassible seaward wall of the endless blackberry forest.

Across the island, an old, battered, hungry fox was startled from its slumbers by Rosamunde's screams. With a shiver, it curled itself into a tighter ball in its warren and dreamed of field mice.

EADWIG ESPINOSA, EALDORMAN OF DAUD

Testimony of Anderey Wanenda, Abbot of Daud

Eadwig Espinosa was already the ealdorman of Daud before I was sent here as a young abbot by the church, and I'm an old man now, so it's frankly hard for me to imagine the shire without him.

He's as much a part of the fabric of our lives as the gloomy weather, the noise and stink of the harbor, and the constant scrabbling to eke out a living wage in this isolated, marshy lowland, which is fundamentally unsuitable for agriculture or animal husbandry. Eadwig is a constant presence, a constant pressure, something inescapable and intractable to be endured, warily. People here think about him the way we think about winter storms off the Eastern Sea: we are watchful of signs and portents, we prepare for the worst, but we know that we're powerless in the face of their full fury, and that no matter how peaceful things may seem at any given moment, it's only a matter of time before that fury is unleashed again, year after year after year.

I walked by the burnt remains of his house this morning on my way to the market, and my first thought was, "Eadwig is certainly going to make somebody pay for this, and I hope that the innocent don't suffer unduly from his wrath." But then, of course, I realized that was just a habitual, conditioned response, since Eadwig's charred remains had been pulled from the smoldering wreckage two weeks ago and quickly interred in the cemetery just outside the shire's north seawall. I performed the rite of burial, of course, as I always do here. Few attended beyond the seven magistrates of the shire, all of whom had been appointed by Eadwig, so I suppose they wanted to see their master off to his great reward. There were no tears shed and no remembrances shared.

Per the shire's ordinances, the magistrates should now be investigating the conflagration that claimed Eadwig's life, so, respectfully, I'm somewhat intrigued that they've brought you here from South Gyrwas to conduct these interviews on their behalf. I suppose the magistrates are self-aware enough to understand that even with Eadwig dead, the people of Daud are going to be loath to speak to them about such matters, knowing how often such past disclosures, intended or inadvertent, often resulted in misfortune once the ealdorman learned of them. It's probably impolitic of me to say so, but I also suspect they're less interested in whether Eadwig's death was a matter of misfortune or misconduct and more interested in which of their number will become the next ealdorman at the Midsummer Council, with Eadwig having left no heir to his hereditary seat.

No acknowledged and accessible heir, anyway, since it's a widely held belief that his former house servant, Jallon Goushe, was his bastard son by Telana Peerat, who used to run a bakery near Eadwig's house. Telana made fine bread, but she was better loved by many in the shire for the strong, dark beer she brewed and surreptitiously sold down at the harbor. She bore Jallon out of wedlock some thirty years ago and refused to publicly identify his father, insinuating by the foreign surname she bestowed upon the child that his sire must have been some sailor not seen again in these parts.

When Jallon was about five years old, the magistrates charged Telana with witchcraft, declaring her brewing skills to be necromantic. She was sentenced by Eadwig to hard labor in the marsh tending the dikes and drowned a few months later, during the Great Flood that submerged the old Outer Daud settlement. I buried her, too.

Eadwig took the boy from the poorhouse where he'd been sent after his mother's conviction and into his own house soon after her death, though he had never exhibited any prior interest in any of the shire's other urchins or orphans nor employed a household servant. The magistrates let it be known that Eadwig simply needed more help about the house as he aged and grew less mobile, and his selection of Jallon was nothing more than a merciful one, demonstrating his benevolence toward those less fortunate than himself. No one else wanted to become even less fortunate than they already were, so the story wasn't challenged at the time, and it's still not often discussed beyond whispers about the hearth.

It's a moot point in any event, since Jallon disappeared after five years or so of visible abuse at Eadwig's hands. Many people believe that Eadwig killed him in a fit of rage, though others say Jallon escaped from Eadwig's home and ran or sailed away to points unknown. Occasionally there are whispers that he's been spotted at the harbor, or hunting in the marshes out beyond the hermitage, or such like.

I don't put much truck in such rumors. Few people ever looked closely at Jallon's dirty face when he was a boy, so I doubt that any of us would recognize him as an adult anyway, nor that he'd be inclined to return to Daud had he successfully escaped. I routinely bury decomposed human remains of unknown provenance found in the marshes, so I strongly suspect that Jallon either was dumped there already dead or drowned there trying to make an escape inland, and he's likely interred in the north seawall cemetery near his former master — or his father, if that's the case.

Which, for the record, I do believe to be the case, based on my long-ago friendship with Telana. I must confess that I adored her beer, an illicit indulgence probably made sweeter by its violation of both my vows and the statutes of prohibition in Daud. I couldn't afford to buy it from her, mind you, but she brought me a jug every now and then as a small token of gratitude, offered in return for my having quietly and privately baptized Jallon as a babe in her arms.

At the time of the baptism, Telana tearfully confided that it was not a consensual coupling that had quickened her womb, though she was afraid to name the man who had forced himself upon her, even to me, even in private. Eadwig and the magistrates are about the only people hereabouts who could inspire such fear, and I know — or knew — all of them well enough to suspect that the ealdorman was the only one temperamentally capable of such a bestial crime. Common people's instincts about such matters are generally sound, if you get my meaning.

Yes, I know that the baptism was both a criminal and heretical act under the ordinances, but it's not the first time, nor likely the last, that I would comfort a faithful woman by gifting her bastard child with some hope for eternal redemption. The Church generally turns the other cheek on such matters in rural outposts like this one, if they're handled quietly and privately. Even Eadwig, stickler that he was for the laws, generally let me be when it came to matters of faith and sacraments.

When the people are comforted with simple promises of eternal life, they're less apt to rise up against their rulers in this life. And that was just fine as far as the old ealdorman was concerned. Just fine, indeed.

Testimony of Dantin Bergeron, Magistrate of Daud

On behalf of all the magistrates of Daud, I want to thank you for traveling from South Gyrwas on such short notice to help us document the facts surrounding Eadwig Espinosa's death. You're a new magistrate yourself in your shire, I understand, and politics being politics, once I tell you what we know and suspect thus far, you'll understand why we sent our messenger to South Gyrwas to call on your ealdorman so soon after Eadwig's death.

For what it's worth, I'm sorry that Ealdorman Tondbert wasn't able to come to our aid himself, but we are all respectfully grateful that he sent you in his stead and relieved that you experienced safe travel between our shires. We've had problems with bandits just outside the watch perimeters, so solo journeys like our messenger's and yours are speedy, if not necessarily the safest choice. At any rate, all niceties aside, I do want to note that we assumed relations between South Gyrwas and Daud had reached an amicable enough point that your fellow magistrates wouldn't feel compelled to keep our messenger in custody in your shire until your safe passage home, but that's a conversation for a different time, I suppose. I trust he's comfortable.

Per our shire's ordinances, as you know, when an ealdorman passes without issue, the next ealdorman will be selected by the magistrates at the Midsummer Council, from among their own number. This election not only will be important to Daud and its people today but could perhaps resonate for generations to come, as the title of ealdorman will again pass from father to son until the line is broken. Eadwig was the ninth ealdorman of the Espinosa line, and the men of his family have generally proven to be long-lived, so it's now been 161 years since the last time an election like this took place.

We're all obviously hopeful that whichever one of us is selected this summer will father a similarly long line of Ealdormen, and I'd be duplicitous if I denied an interest in being the first of many Bergerons to lead our shire. As would any of the other six magistrates, who are equally ambitious in such matters — but we all understand that the council will not adjourn until the seven of us can successfully select one of our number with at least a four-to-three majority, so there will be plenty of horse-trading and promise-making in the months between now and Midsummer.

As exciting as such matters are to us all, we also have other, more pressing affairs to attend to, so let me advise you on what we know about Eadwig's death. Most importantly, it is clear to us that the fire that consumed the Ealdorman's home was purposefully set, most likely by someone who had access to and familiarity with the manor house. Eyewitness reports and a cursory walk of the site after the fire indicate that the two stairwells on either side of the great kitchen complex seemed to be alight before the rest of the house went up in flames, blocking any access or egress to the second floor, where Eadwig worked and slept. And died, as it happens.

Early respondents to the fire also reported a strong smell of fish oil about the house as it burned, so we suspect that substance was used as to fuel the blaze. Eadwig would have had plenty of fish oil in his pantry to fuel his lamps, of course, but there were no explosions, as one would expect if whole barrels of the stuff had been ignited by an encroaching accidental fire. That leads us to believe that fish oil was dumped onto rags or other debris and lit at the bottom of the stairwells, which were lined with tapestries that would have readily carried the blazes upward.

While it must be considered as part of your due diligence, the magistrates consider suicide highly unlikely in this case, not just as a matter of its improbability, given Eadwig's temperament, but also as a matter of logistics. The ealdorman's charred body was found amid furniture from the second floor of his house, which collapsed to ground level once the blaze consumed the structural beams. It's difficult to imagine the elderly Eadwig — who was physically frail at age ninety-two, despite his fierce temper and sharp mental acuity — lighting a fire at the base of one stairwell, ascending to the second floor, walking the length of the house, descending to the ground level at the opposite end, lighting another fire, then ascending again and walking back to his bedroom near the midline of the house to await his demise.

So if the fire that took Eadwig's life was neither an unfortunate accident nor suicide, then we're left with but one explanation for the events of that night: Eadwig Espinosa was murdered in his own home, in a coldly premeditated and calculated fashion. Our eyes and ears about the shire report that this is already the commonest-held belief of the people — and that they consider the likeliest suspects for the crime to be among the people who had the most frequent and visible access to Eadwig's house: us, the magistrates, who are, somewhat rightly, also perceived as having the most to gain from his death.

This is why you're here, ultimately, since we want to dispel any worries among the people that one of us will become ealdorman through acts of skullduggery. We believe that an independent investigation by a friendly ealdorman from another shire — or his designee, as it turns out — is the best way to alleviate questions about our interests and integrity in this matter.

The current citizenry is, quite frankly, cowed after decades of strong rule by Eadwig, so we're not so much worried about them today as we are looking to the future, reducing the likelihood that the chosen line will be challenged in years to come as illegitimate by virtue of being rooted in nefarious acts. History is funny, as you know, and a time may come when people look back on Eadwig Espinosa as a sage and successful ealdorman who maintained the peace in unpeaceful times, and there's no sense leaving a mystery surrounding his death to fester for generations.

So who, then, killed Eadwig Espinosa? We hope you can divine the answer to this mystery, and we've issued you a warrant that will entitle you to speak with anyone in the shire, ourselves included, and to have access to any homes, properties, or places to which your inquiries may lead you.

I'll be blunt on one point: There is no shortage of suspects, since pretty much everybody in the shire has some reason to be angry with or aggrieved by Eadwig. The old ealdorman ruled by intimidation, and he meted out capital punishments — either directly, by hanging, or indirectly, by servitude on the dikes or other hard labors — with zeal and alacrity.

It's a rare family in Daud today that hasn't lost at least one member in the past half-century to Eadwig's enthusiastic embrace of his judicial authority. Including my own, I should note: shortly after Eadwig appointed me to serve as a magistrate, he had my uncle Ranelf Bergeron, a simple fisherman, hanged for conspiracy to commit maritime theft. I believe that was intended to send a message to me about just how far my authority did and didn't extend. Most of the other magistrates will report similar events in their own families. And if you believe one of the longstanding stories that floats about the shire, the list of families victimized by Eadwig's spite includes even the Espinosas, as the old man once employed an orphaned houseboy who many people believe was his bastard and whose eventual disappearance was whispered to be at Eadwig's own hand.

I mention that because I know you'll hear about it as you make your inquiries about the shire. There's nothing to the story, as best I can see. The boy's name was Jallon Goushe. His mother was a witch who whored at the harbor, and Eadwig sent her to the dikes, then took her boy as a servant after she died there. While I'll admit it seemed odd and somewhat out of character at the time, I know that Eadwig needed more help about his house as he aged, and he likely just selected an orphan at random from the poorhouse, one being just as good as any other, equally capable of emptying his piss pot and wiping the street grime from his windows.

I will also note that, if nothing else, Eadwig was cautious about covering his tracks and judicious about having others handle the dirtiest of his work, so if he'd wanted the boy dead, he'd have made a public spectacle of it within the confines of the ordinances and not done it quietly and mysteriously, even in a rage. The other magistrates and I are confident that Jallon fled Eadwig's house and Daud, despite what the people hereabouts might tell you. Eadwig's monstrosities were always executed within the constraints of the shire's ordinances. Always.

After Jallon fled, Eadwig never took in another permanent servant. He has employed a housekeeper named Makvala Janzen in recent years, but she doesn't live in his house, she just visits — or visited, rather — a few times each week to tend to necessary household matters for him. Makvala's a well-regarded crone who was widowed young when her husband went down in the Eastern Sea in a storm. She works as a cook and laundress at the poorhouse where she lives, and she does a little bit of this and that for some of the magistrates and our wives, and Abbot Anderey, and a few others, Eadwig included, obviously.

She's trustworthy and is one of the few people in the shire who isn't widely damned in the eyes of the common folk by her proximity to Eadwig. I'd certainly recommend speaking to Makvala, though I doubt that she'll tell you anything, and no one suspects her of being involved with the fires or knowledgeable of the person or persons who set them. But maybe she saw something that would be helpful to you, who knows?

As I think about it, not having a live-in servant like Jallon probably contributed to Eadwig's demise, since had there been another person in the house when the fires began, that person could have perhaps staved the blazes off, or sounded a more timely warning, or helped Eadwig to escape the inferno. I'd call that a pity, since all of the magistrates would have preferred it if Jallon or Makvala or somebody else had saved Eadwig, so that he could have died a quiet death in his sleep some time later.

Not because he deserved such a peaceful departure, mind you, but rather because we'd prefer to select the next ealdorman without a cloud of uncertainty and suspicion hanging over our heads. But that's Eadwig's final gift to us all, I suppose. Very much in keeping with all the ones that came before it, I'd say.

Testimony of Fennegren Peerat, Blacksmith

I need to make one thing clear right now: I had no beef with Eadwig Espinosa. He let me be, and I let him be, and I had nothing to do with the fire that burned him up. So I don't know why you need to talk to me, even though I respect the warrant you showed me from the magistrates that says you can ask me what you want, and I'm bound to answer. So I'll do that, but I had nothing to do with any of this, and I don't know anybody who did.

Yes, Telana Peerat was my sister. Yes, she's dead. Yes, Eadwig Espinosa sent her to work on the dikes, and she drowned there. Why? She was charged with witchcraft because she made beer, and turning one thing into another is considered necromancy. No, I don't see it that way, but Eadwig did, and beer is illegal in Daud anyway. That was his job. It's not my place to question. Yes, I miss her, but I guess she got what she deserved. That's not for me to say.

Yes, I am a blacksmith. Yes, I've done work for Eadwig. Horseshoes. Door hinges and latches. Buckles. Yes, I've also sold him soap, which I make when I am able and when I have the materials for it. Yes, I sell it at the market or down at the harbor, not here in the shop. For extra money, yes. Well, yes, you're right about that, soap is just like beer, it's one thing made when other things change form and take on new powers. It runs in our family, I guess. No, I hadn't thought about it like that, but I suppose that, yes, I could have been charged with necromancy, too. Why not? Probably because Eadwig liked soap and didn't like beer, I guess. Or because one's legal to have and one isn't. I don't know. Maybe I was just lucky. It's not my place to know such things. No, I don't know.

Yes, Telana had a son. No, I don't know who the father was. She sold beer at the harbor, and sailors can be rough, so I guess one of them forced himself on her. No, I did not take care of her son when she was sent away to the dikes. Because I have no wife, and I thought he'd be better cared for by the crones at the poorhouse. I already had an apprentice, yes. No, Telana's boy was too young and small to be of use in my smithy, and I could not have afforded to feed him. Yes,

Eadwig did take him in after Tclana died. No, I don't know why. No, I don't know what happened to him. No, I don't think he is still alive.

No, I don't think Eadwig killed him. Why would you ask me such a thing? I think that the boy ran away from his master, and in trying to avoid the guard post on the road to South Gyrwas, he ventured into the marshes and drowned. He was about ten years old, I guess. When what, born or disappeared? Oh, I guess it's been about twenty years since he's been gone.

No, I don't really remember what he looked like, and I wouldn't recognize him. He was a dirty little boy, like all the other dirty little boys in Daud. A lot of them die or disappear. That's life here. I don't pay much attention to them until they're old enough to buy my wares.

Yes, I suppose it could have been different in this case, since he was my sister's boy. But she was charged with witchcraft, and its taint would stick to her son through her adultery, you understand? I wanted no part of that. No, I don't think I had an obligation to him. Not to her, either.

I said I don't know who his father was. Yes, I know what some people say. Some people should keep their mouths shut. Yes, I have been in Eadwig's house. I hung some doors for him, after he bought latches and hinges from me. I do that for a lot of people. No, they were not doors to the outside. No, I don't remember my way around the house.

Yes, I saw the stairs. I went up them to hang one of the doors. Which one? What do you mean? There are two stairwells in the house? I didn't see the other one, then. Yes, the one by the kitchen. At the east end.

Yes, I do use fish oil when I make soap, since you have to have a fat, and that's obviously easier to come by here than goat or other animal tallow. Do I have any now? No, I don't. I buy or trade for it when I can, and when I get enough of it, then I make a batch. I made and sold some a few months back, and haven't had time since. No, I don't use it in lamps. When the sun goes down, I stoke my forge if I want to see something, and I go to sleep if I don't.

No, I don't have anything else to say. No, I don't know who else you should talk to. No, I will not remember anything else later. Yes, I am sure.

Testimony of Makvala Janzen, Widow and Laundress

So the house matron tells me you're from South Gyrwas, are you? I wouldn't have guessed that. I sailed there a few times as a pretty young woman with my husband on his fishing boat, and I've met a lot of Gyrwan sailors down at the harbor, and you don't have the accent I associate with folks from that shire, do you? You must have had good schooling, eh? You speak almost as well as we Daudans do, don't you, ha? You do, you do! But no matter, I'm sorry to natter on. Old women hear things funny sometimes, don't we?

Well, I see you have a warrant from the magistrates, so you're here to question me, aren't you? About Old Eadwig, I'll bet, hmm? Not much else of excitement happening in Daud that would merit someone of your standing paying a visit to an old woman like me, is there? No, no, there's not. And while I'm honored by your presence here — since we don't get visitors of your caliber here at the poor house very often, do we, no? — I think you must understand that the way a poor, old lady like me gets to work in fine houses like Eadwig's is by seeing nothing, and then talking about that nothing even less, yes?

I'd certainly like to keep cleaning the magistrates' houses to take the burden off their poor, lovely wives, and if they heard I was telling a stranger — even a fine, gentle one with a fine, fancy warrant like you — secrets about old Eadwig, well, they'd soon see fit to hire a new housekeeper, wouldn't they? They don't pay me much, but every penny helps, and I share a bit of my earnings when I'm able with the little ones here at the poorhouse, which so brightens their days, doesn't it? It would be a shame to disappoint the little ones here, wouldn't it? I'd say so, certainly, yes, it would. What a pity, no?

So if it pleases you, good sir from Gyrwas, all I'd like to say about the unfortunate events at Eadwig's house is that I visited him two days before the fire, and saw nothing awry or different than I'd seen any other day that I was there. It wasn't the kind of house where things changed very often, was it? Old Eadwig was set in his ways, and he liked things the way he liked them, and if I'd seen anything different from how it should have been, why, I'd have just cleaned it up and put it back the right way without a second thought, wouldn't I, yes?

And since I didn't see anything, did I, then, well, I can't very well offer a guess on who would have done such a thing or why, can I? Old Eadwig had a job to do, and he did it. It didn't make him popular, did it? But I'm not so sure that it should have. Why, if being ealdorman was a pageant for the popular, then we'd have to pick a new one every year, people being fickle as they are, aren't they? And that would never do, would it? No sir, it wouldn't. Old Eadwig didn't ask to be ealdorman, did he? He was born to it, just like the rest of us are born to our lot. I suspect he did the best he could under the circumstances, didn't he?

What's that? His boy? Well, sir, I've got to shake a finger at the person who told you that tale, don't I? It's idle chatter for fishwives, not something for you to write on your papers there, is it? Yes, I knew young Jallon, you knew that, didn't you? He lived in the poorhouse too, after his mother was sent to the dikes and before Old Eadwig took him away. He was a smart boy, well taught by his ma'am, kind to the other urchins, wasn't he? He was confident, too. Stood out from the others, didn't he? Straight up. Looked you in the eye. Bright. It didn't surprise me at all that old Eadwig picked him out when he came looking for a boy to help him about his house, did it?

Pity about him running off though, wasn't it? Most folks think he probably drowned in the marshes, and in this case, I suspect that most folks are right, aren't they? Some may tell you that old Eadwig killed the boy, but you shouldn't listen to that, never mind write it down, should you? If the old man had wanted Jallon dead and gone for some reason, then there'd have been no mystery, since it would have happened out in the open, official, you might say, the way all the other things like that happened, you understand?

And it didn't happen that way, did it? No. No, it did not, hmm?

Report of Copico Warosa, Magistrate of South Gyrwas

Good evening, friend magistrates of Daud. I want to thank you, first, for providing me and my ealdorman, Goodman Tondbert Aethelred, with the opportunity to show South Gyrwas' deep regard for the people of Daud by assisting you with your investigation into the death of your ealdorman. As magistrates, we have a deep responsibility to our people to enforce ordinances, evaluate incidents, and make recommendations to our ealdormen regarding redress or punishment, as appropriate and applicable. One of you is expected to become the new ealdorman of Daud in a few months, and I understand clearly how important it is that you plainly document and share the facts associated with Eadwig's death, to remove any stain of impropriety against your next ealdorman and his heirs.

Truth, as you know, can be difficult to divine, and is often dependent upon the prejudices and perspectives of both the narrator and the listener in any exchange. Both can be untrustworthy, especially with regard to points of passion, or remembrances of rarely seen incidents, or when there are unequal interests and powers represented between the parties in the conversation.

While I have found the people of Daud to be wary with strangers — especially strangers with warrants — I do believe for the most part that they answered my questions as truthfully as they were able. That being said, those truths were not always consonant with each other, since we view the world and events around us through the lenses of our own wants, needs, and experiences, so one person's reality does not necessarily correspond to another's. Thus, my role as the investigator is to knit such disparate, subjective, personal narratives together into a single objective story and to find the truth, singular, that answers the question, singular, at hand, no matter how unpleasant or remarkable or illuminating or disappointing or surprising said truth might be.

And with that as preamble, I would like to report that it is my deeply held and final opinion that Eadwig was a victim of death by misfortune, with the fire that destroyed his home and took his life being of accidental origin. While many anecdotal observations were shared by you and your people regarding revenge motives, the smell of fish oil, and the apparently purposeful burning of nonadjacent stairwells, I can find no compelling evidence of conspiracy or individual malfeasance to declare that evening's events as anything other than an unfortunate accident.

Embers can smolder in walls behind hearths and cooking stoves, often for surprisingly long times, days even, before they reach a point where they burn through, encounter fresh air, and leap into active blazes. With Eadwig's kitchen situated along the back wall of his house, between the stairwells, it's likely that a spark or heat from the cooking stove ignited an ember in one of the voids behind the wall or in the ceiling's wooden panels. This smoldering, incipient flame likely crept along unseen and unnoticed toward one stairwell, ignited violently upon exposure to fresh air, forcing flames back through the crevices to the stairwell at the other end of the house, firing the tapestries there as well.

Given the proximity of Eadwig's house to the harbor, I think the most likely explanation of the fish oil smell is simply that the odors of the ships lining the wharves and their fulsome cargoes were pulled toward the scene by the strong, upward-flowing winds that always surround large, burning fires like this one. Had Eadwig lived closer to the inland side of the shire, I believe people would have reported a smell of marsh gas instead.

I understand that you and some of your people would have preferred a more dramatic outcome to my investigation, but the explanation for extraordinary events is often mundane. I am certain that is the case here — and equally certain that you would have come to the same conclusion had the victim of the fire been some peasant or fishmonger and had his death not had such a profound impact on your own future fortunes.

I have documented my findings, so that you may share them as you see fit with your people. I hope this will be sufficient to allow your next ealdorman to assume his new role freed from any taint or suspicion, now or in the years and generations that follow. With that, I consider this investigation closed and will ride for South Gyrwas this afternoon. Your messenger should return to Daud by week's end, assuming neither of us encounters bandits or other scoundrels along the way.

Again, thank you for the opportunity to cement the bonds between our shires, and best wishes to you all in the months and years ahead, especially as you choose your new ealdorman at the Midsummer Council. May your next line of ealdormen rule as long as the Espinosas!

Two Weeks Later: Report of Calman Starde, Highway Watch Captain

We found the body of the messenger of Daud yesterday while on patrol just outside of the watch perimeter, in a brushy, dry clearing on the north side of the road. He had been run through the gut with a sharp fireplace poker, bearing a crest that I know to be that of the House of Epinosa. The messenger's belly was hugely distended when we found him, which seemed odd at this cold time of the year. When we moved him, a strong viscous fluid, which smelt and felt like fish oil, rushed out of his mouth and wounds.

A letter from the magistrates to Ealdorman Tondbert of South Gyrwas was still in the messenger's pouch, though its seal had been broken. The messenger also carried a variety of local coins and small trade goods in his pouch, and none of the unique coins and objects that travelers typically carry when returning from South Gyrwas. This makes it clear to us that the messenger was waylaid while outbound, and not on returning, meaning that he never arrived at his appointed destination, nor delivered his message to its intended audience.

Given what I now understand has occurred here in the shire while we were on the perimeter, it seems apparent that whoever killed the messenger likely assumed the role of a magistrate of South Gyrwas and conducted an investigation into Ealdorman Eadwig's death under false pretense. Presumably, we must call into question that investigation's findings, given the circumstances.

I cannot fathom why someone would do such a thing, nor why the messenger would have been force-fed a toxic quantity of fish oil and then speared through with an item apparently stolen from the Ealdorman's home before the recent fire. Was it all out of spite? Some cruel entertainment? Was it an odd act of war, or the act of a madman?

Or does somebody out there somewhere simply want to send his own message to the magistrates and people of Daud? If so, it doesn't seem to be a friendly one, does it?

I LIE ON MY BACK IN THE GRASS, AND I LOOK AT THE SUN

I lie on my back in the grass, and I look at the sun.

The sun explodes, but I don't know it until eight minutes and twenty seconds later, owing to the great distance between our star and me.

I possess that knowledge for only thirteen milliseconds.

ଓଓଓଓଓ

I lie on my back in the grass, and I look at the sun.

Teresa lies next to me, mouth slightly agape as she slumbers in post-lunch languor, anesthetized by the lovely warmth of the cloudless day. I turn and smile in her direction, noting that she is truly as beautiful as she was on the day that I first laid eyes on her, all those years ago, on an equally glorious and sunny day.

I had docked my small boat in the city harbor after a day on the lake and was storing my sails and lines when a larger (objectively) and nicer (subjectively) boat cruised by my slip under motor power, Teresa sunbathing on the foredeck, leaning against the windows of the cockpit. I am not normally a gawker, at all, but I admit that I did stand up specifically to admire her beauty for a bit longer as her boat passed, and she caught me, tipping her head down, looking over her sunglasses, and flashing me a half-smile.

I smiled back, feeling caught and bashful, and returned to my chores, but I surreptitiously watched her boat moor, watched who got off it (Teresa, two men — one older and one younger — and a garrulous-looking, blond Labrador-type dog, none of whom seemed to obviously and overtly belong to her, if little cues of affection and possession were to be trusted), and watched where they went: the harbor patio bar. Just as I'm not normally a gawker, at all, I'm also not normally a flirter, but for some reason that I can't quite explain, perhaps just emboldened by the beauty of the day, I strolled to the harbor patio some fifteen minutes later, elbowed my way to the bar next to her party (she was on the left-hand side), and made eye contact. She smiled again — electrifying — and asked if I was following her.

I admitted that I was. She laughed, and introduced herself, and then she introduced me to her brother, her father, and his dog, Maxwell. I ordered a drink. She already had one. Then I ordered another, plus one for her. Then her brother bought drinks for us all. Maxwell rubbed against my legs, demanding pets and pats, and eventually plopped down, panting, at my feet.

"He likes you," Teresa's father said. "That means you must be good people."

As the sun set, we moved to a table with an umbrella and ordered dinner and talked about the types of things that people who don't really know each other typically talk about. Then her brother left, and then her father and Maxwell left, and then, much later, Teresa and I left together. We have spent very few days apart since then, in sickness and in health, through thick and through thin, for better and for worse. She looks so peaceful today. That's a good thing to see.

Our appointment with the divorce attorney is in thirty minutes.

ଔଔଔଔଔ

I lie on my back in the grass, and I look at the sun.

The sailors move about on the beach below me, and I can see them out of the corner of my eye as they pass across my limited field of vision, hauling plantains and coconuts and cut logs from a pile they'd stored at the edge of the woods, through the low waves, and onto the shallow dinghies that will shuttle the goods to the caravel they've anchored beyond the reef.

They arrived a week or so ago, and we watched them as they clattered about our island in their ridiculous armor, clearly enjoying being ashore after untold weeks at sea and clearly pleased by the bounty of our land. They would occasionally notice us and speak in what appeared to be admiring tones, though none of us could actually understand what they were communicating. We just went about our business, as we always do, eating, drinking, basking, mating, laying eggs, sleeping.

Things changed yesterday: with no advance warning, groups of sailors began roughly rounding dozens of us up, the larger ones among us requiring two or three men to move us against our wills. We tucked our heads and feet and tails into our shells, protecting ourselves against harm, as we always do, but that actually seemed to make it easier for the sailors to roll us over onto our backs and haul us on our carapaces down to the grassy strip before the beach.

I've been lying here on my back since then. I feel nauseous and disoriented and dizzy in equal measure, since my insides are not accustomed to supporting my outsides in this absurd configuration. Occasionally I'll push out my feet, or stretch my neck, or extend my tail, as we always do, but it's more out of frustration than anything else, since I know full well that I can't turn myself over and escape. None of the others can, either. So I just watch the sun cross the sky, and I wait for what will come, as we always do.

The pile of goods at the edge of the woods is gone now, and the sun has dropped close to the horizon. As best I can see from this disadvantaged viewpoint, we're the only things left on the grassy knoll above the beach.

Rough hands suddenly grab my shell from behind and begin hauling me down the slope to the boats. I close my eyes and retreat within my shell, as we always do.

☙☙☙☙☙

I lie on my back in the grass and I look at the sun.

I do my best thinking this way, warmed and invigorated by those most elemental solar forces — both waves and particles, simultaneously — which make possible everything we are, have ever been, and will ever be. Our sun is the grandest object that we tiny humans can directly and intimately experience; there are greater stars, of course, but they are too far away for us to apprehend their majesty, and there are closer objects also, of course, but none with the heft (literal and figurative) of our central star. It makes life possible, and life makes thought possible, and thought makes everything possible.

I've spent most of my adult life pondering some the cosmos' most inexplicable puzzles, seeking to tease order from chaos, then to communicate that order in ways that other people can understand, ideally to inspire them to think of similar matters, perchance to discover their own solutions or divine their own secrets, which they, in turn, can pass along to others. We are smarter collectively than we are individually, which is why I always keep a journal with me to record my thoughts, the better to share them when the chance presents itself, or to record the wisdom of others when it is presented to me.

Knowledge is additive, but the only way to increase the sum of knowledge is to be able to fully define both the augend (that which is known) and the addend (that which accrues to the augend) before applying a Boolean "and" function to merge them into something greater than before. If either of those elements is "unknown" or "uncertain," then applying any additive or conjunctive operations to it will produce only "unknown" or "uncertain" as a result; so we can't add to knowledge until we know all the knowledge that exists to date. The absence of the knowledge of all knowledge (knowledge-plex) is akin to multiplying by zero; everything is negated by the incomplete set, no matter how large or small it might be. Absence always subtracts or divides, never adds or multiplies.

So I spend many, many, many hours in the libraries of this great city working to build a complete and thorough augend of all knowledge known to be known before me, so that I may apply my own insightful addends to make that plurality greater still, just as the sun absorbs the comets and planetoids and extrasolar objects that drop into it, nearly continually, tiny drops in a stream that eventually builds an ocean, made of light, both waves and particles, simultaneously. It takes eight minutes and twenty seconds for light to travel from the sun to earth. It takes more time for it to go the other way, because it's fighting the current.

Occasionally I have insights that are not only additive but multiplicative, so I convert my augend of knowledge to a multiplicand through deft use of both associative and commutative laws, and by equally skillful application of my innovative multipliers, I am able to catapult heavy chunks of knowing farther, faster, than has ever happened before, achieving breakthroughs of great eloquence and beauty. Whenever such insightful explosions flash like supernovae across the crystalline lattice of neurons within my skull, I mouth a quiet "thank you" to my most admired predecessor, the greatest Scot himself, James Clerk Maxwell, whose classic theory of electromagnetic radiation integrated electricity, magnetism, and light as manifestations of the same phenomenon, simultaneously.

Maxwell was wise, certainly, but absent the overarching view of all known knowledge that my libraries afford me, he missed several crucial points about the ways in which heat, time, life, thought, and faith are also manifestations of those same primal phenomena, all of them fueled by the stars in the heavens, creating the lattice-like crystalline structures that frame the cosmos and along which we all could travel, if only we could fully deploy the power of faith, which is entangled at a quantum level with thought, which is entangled at a nuclear level with life, which is entangled at a molecular level with time, which is entangled at a cellular level with heat, which stems from the sun, carrying electricity, magnetism, and light as it rockets about the cosmos, more rapidly than Einstein's *c*, more constantly than Euler's *e*, more patiently than Avogadro's N_A, more transcendental than Catalan's *G*, more . . .

What? I wasn't shouting. No, I wasn't. This park is public. You already told me I couldn't block the pavement outside of the library, so I came here. Where do you want me to go? Don't you have anything better to do than to harass me while I'm thinking? Speeding tickets? Stopping murders? Something? No. No. I'm moving. I've already read all the books in the shelter library, and the county jail library, too. I don't need to go there again. Just let me collect my things . . . it won't take long . . . do you see my journals anywhere?

ও৪ও৪ও৪ও৪ও৪

I lie on my back in the grass, and I look at the sun.

It's quite bright, and I've lost the ability to blink, so I suspect it will blind me shortly. My eyes are burning already. I don't appear to be able to generate tears anymore.

We landed on the island last week, looking for turtles. Their meat is succulent, and they last for months on the ship, as long as you keep them on their backs and toss salt water on them every now and then.

We've landed on six islands over the past few months which were rich with terrapins and scant with humans, so I suppose that caused us to lower our guard and grow careless.

I was picking bananas when I felt the sting of an arrow pierce my armor between the neck and breast plates, where a leather sleeve allows motion but reduces protection. I pulled the offending shaft from my upper chest and smiled despite the sting; not much of an arrow really, more like a primitive dart. It would take more than that to fell a Spaniard!

But, alas, I grinned too soon: apparently the dart was treated with some nefarious poison, and I began to seize and stumble within minutes of being struck, tottering into an open field, where I fell on my back, and have not been able to rise again.

The sun is quite bright today, and I cannot close my eyes against it. I've been saying mental prayers to Teresa of Ávila, the patron saint of my people, that my end might be quick and painless. I suspect I am to be disappointed in terrible ways, though, since it seems the poison only affects the muscles associated with external motion, not my heart and my breathing, so I may lie here for a long, long while, unless one of my shipmates finds me.

I won't be able to explain what happened, though, nor ask him to kill me as a mercy, because I can't speak either, nor even swallow for that matter. Maybe I will drown in my own spit before I roast under the tropical sun or am flayed alive by the savages who shot me.

I think I hear one of them now, coming through the forest.

ᏨᏨᏨᏨᏨ

I lie on my back in the grass, and I look at the sun.

This is my favorite spot on our estate, a quiet, remote corner against the forest, beyond the hay field, where the hill slopes upward to the west.

I can understand why my ancestors chose to put their burial ground here. Stones mark the spots where my parents, my grandparents, my great-grandparents, and assorted cousins, neighbors, friends, and acquaintances were laid when their times under the sun came to an end, and they were consigned to the earth from which we all once sprang and to which we all must return.

The freshest graves are at the east end of the plot, though the grass has grown to cover them, and the mounded soil has settled back into place, so you'd not quickly know they were new if you didn't read the little dated stones at their heads.

One says "Maxwell." He was my dog. A good boy, he was. Fine companion, excellent judge of people. I trusted him implicitly. If he liked you, I liked you.

The other one says "Baby." He was my grandson, stillborn. My daughter, Teresa, could not bring herself to record a name on his stone, as if that would have magnified and multiplied her grief, somehow, by personalizing it, forever.

Her husband couldn't and can't seem to understand this; they had picked a name for the boy, as parents always do, and he has always referred to their lost one by that name, which my daughter has never spoken since his birth and death, to the best of my knowledge. He is smart in so many ways, but an idiot in this regard.

It's been two years since we buried the boy, and the brittleness between Teresa and her husband has grown rather than abated over that time. It's heartbreaking for me to watch. I suspect their marriage may not survive.

Poor Baby. Poor Maxwell. Poor Teresa.

ଓଓଓଓଓ

I lie on my back in the grass, and I look at the sun.

All of the other I's lie on all of the other grasses and look at all of the other suns, I and I and I's minds quantum-entangled in real time across the parsecs that separate I from I and I, and I and I and I from the central mind on Maxwell's Star in Galactic Center, where the Order of Saint Teresa is headquartered, and where I and I and I were encoded before we were sent to do the saint's bidding.

I see a small yellow sun, relatively young, relatively stable, and without stellar companions of note. Other I's see giant, red stars; cold, brown stars; tiny, blue stars; quiescent, white stars; and countless combinations thereof. I and I and I are resting now, absorbing energy from these suns via radiant armor collectors, recovering from the travails associated with transiting cometary and planetary belts en route to I and I and I's staging sites. The signal noise and rocky nuggets surrounding these outlying stars are fatiguing, even for I and I and I.

Soon I and I and I will rise, restored, and begin the final phase of this mission, launching from the refueling planets to plummet into their suns, where I and I and I will simultaneously detonate the thermo-photo-magneto faith bomb entombed in each I's heart, and fueled via Saint Teresa's Fire, which courses along the cosmos's crystal latticework, and upon which I and I and I have ridden from Maxwell's Star.

I and I and I are on one of the largest decontamination missions of the current epoch, and when this work is complete, I and I and I will have cleared an entire galactic arm of the parasitic organisms that have colonized it, polluting it with subfaith thought mass and self-reproducing toxic-organic slurries and pre-entanglement hives and nests.

When my assigned sun explodes, I shall ride its freed energy home, with nary a rocky nugget in the lattice to impede my exuberant, joyful, triumphant progress.

ଓଓଓଓଓ

I lie on my back in the grass, and I look at the sun.

It is very, very bright today.

I turn over on my belly and enjoy the feel of the cool greenery against my cheek.

THE PASSION OF O'WAYNE ALGER

O'Wayne Alger was the greatest VektorSchift player who had ever passed through the flickering neon portal of the Quemby Mall GameStation. His finesse with the twinjet firing buttons (left and right thumbs equally agile), ability to deftly manage the bilateral navigation toggles with only his ring and little fingers, skill at sequentially punching moonchild, sus-tayn-z, and polygroon buttons without removing his eyes from the game screen, and an uncanny immobility that allowed him to balance soda cans and Chik-O-Fill sandwiches on his ample thighs while seated on a stool before the console made him a legend among the arcade's regulars.

The game's "Superior VektorSchift Warriors" screen was always filled with ten of his scores, tagged "OWA," and had the screen recorded the top 100 scores, the vast majority of them would have read "OWA" as well. No one else could even get close to O'Wayne Alger's persistence and quality of play, and he had personally experienced game levels that less seasoned players considered mythical until they beheld them with their own eyes over their master's sloping, dandruff-flecked shoulders.

The VektorSchift console video game was reported in trade magazines to have one hundred levels of play, and the highest "OWA" scores were generally achieved on levels ninety-eight and ninety-nine. This proximity to perfection fostered great speculation and excitement among the Quemby

Mall GameStation community as to what might happen when O'Wayne finally beat level one hundred, since there were no known accounts of that epic summit's having been scaled in any GameStation franchise around the state.

Attendance at the Quemby Mall GameStation rose visibly when O'Wayne was present at the console. This required Roger Evers, the arcade's manager, to strictly enforce a "play to stay" rule, thereby ensuring that quarters flowed into the other machines, since once O'Wayne sat down, the take on the VektorSchift machine was going to be negligible for the remainder of the evening. It was understood by all players present that a wasted quarter or three pumped into a lame, second-tier game that you deliberately played slowly and could walk away from if needed was a fair price to pay for the chance to witness history, whenever it finally happened.

Occasionally, a new or oblivious customer would be playing the arcade's sole VektorSchift machine when O'Wayne arrived after his shift at the Chik-O-Fill on the other side of the mall's central courtyard, and a vast hush would fall across the gaming room while O'Wayne waited. The psychic energy behind that silence would invariably unsettle the offending player, causing him to inadvertently self-detonate a thrakmagnet or steer his Kudusai Klipper into the side of a Starless Barge or fire his thrangozibulx into the poop-end of a wormhole, setting off antimatter waves that obliterated all available lives.

O'Wayne didn't speak much, outside of taking orders at the Chik-O-Fill, but he was well aware of (and quietly pleased by) the awe in which he was held by his peers, and he devoted a sizable amount of time and effort away from the VektorSchift console to honing routines, recording exploits, and formulating gameplay strategies to preserve that potent air of prestige.

It was, in fact, this dedication to his craft that led directly to his untimely demise. He was scribbling notes in his pocket pad while walking home from Quemby Mall one dark February night after a level ninety-seven b'boombot had unexpectedly vrooomed his blastic rhino, and he did not notice that the lights at the corner had changed before stepping out onto Brondesbury Road. A delivery truck (for a sandwich shop that competed with Chik-O-Fill, as it turned out) attempted to stop in time to avoid the unexpected and distracted pedestrian, but an unfortunately situated sheet of black ice caused the truck to slide directly into O'Wayne Alger at speed, snuffing the life of the unfortunate gamer before he even hit the pavement, twenty yards away.

The local newspaper reported the tragedy two days later (O'Wayne had died after the first day's print deadline), and his brief, staff-penned obituary included quotes from two fellow GameStation patrons and O'Wayne's shift manager at Chik-O-Fill, all describing what a fine human being he'd been: quiet, humble, focused, hardworking, dependable, and solid. Readers learned that O'Wayne Alger had been raised in foster homes after his mother had given him up for adoption soon after his birth and that, as a result, he had no known relatives, nor alumni friends, since he'd never graduated from high school or college.

Twenty-seven people attended his memorial service (twenty-two of them regular patrons of the Quemby Mall

GameStation), and thirteen of those traveled on to the crematory where O'Wayne's mortal remains were returned to ashes and dust, once and for all.

And then everyone else went home.

ᏣᏣᏣᏣᏣ

Well, *that* was weird . . .

I had just stepped off the curb to cross Brondesbury Road on my way home from Quemby Mall, with my hoodie cinched up around my head to protect me from the winter wind. I couldn't see very well, but it didn't really matter, since my eyes were focused on my shivering hands before me as I was trying to finish a three-dimensional doodle in my pocket notepad showing the path of an unexpected b'boombot as it had traversed the Ginjeet Dome on level ninety-seven, werning my Kudusai Klipper but good. Then I felt a hard and sudden shove on my left side, and a second later, I found myself standing in front of the VektorSchift console at the GameStation, staring at the "Superior VektorSchift Warriors" screen, which showed my ten "OWA" top scores.

That was a pleasant thing to look at, sure, but unexpected. How had I suddenly ended up here? Had I blacked out and walked back to the mall? Or had I stumbled into the food-end of a real-life wormhole that had its poop-end right here in front of the VektorSchift console? Stranger things have happened, I guess.

I looked away from the console screen. The ceiling lights of the arcade were off, and the metal doors to the

Quemby Mall central courtyard were closed as well. Still weird. But then I figured that when things got weird, then the weird got . . . uhhhh . . . things. So I figured I might as well stick with what I knew to see what happened next, and I sat down on my stool and fished in my pocket for a quarter to run through a bonus late-night VektorSchift game.

Except that I didn't have any pockets, or any quarters, or any hands, for that matter. I could see a shimmery outline of my own shape, and my left hand and arm seemed to be a bit *squished*, for lack of a better word. I reached up for the VektorSchift console and was shocked when my hands weren't able to grasp the joysticks or press the buttons but just seemed to pass through or around them, somehow. This was serious!

I jumped up from the VektorSchift game and straightaway walked toward the metal screen at the entry to the arcade. I reached for the grated gate, but my hands passed straight through the steel panels, too, and try as I might, I couldn't grasp the handle. Even weirder. And kind of scary.

Since my hands were passing clear through the metal locking mechanism of the gate, I decided to push my arms through the grate as well, and they went through, unimpeded. I carefully stepped forward, my whole body passing through the supposedly solid and secure metal gate, and I found myself standing in the kitchen area of the Chik-O-Fill where I worked — one step taking me between those points, never mind the fact that there should have been an entire central mall courtyard between them.

I paced around the Chik-O-Fill kitchen and then walked out into the dining area. I couldn't grasp the locked doors into the mall atrium of the Chik-O-Fill either, but when I walked, eyes open, straight through the wall, I found myself transported to my basement apartment at 475 Marine Road. I tried to open the door of the apartment, failed, then pushed myself through the door and ended up back on the GameStation floor, in front of the VektorSchift machine.

I repeated this sequence several times, pushing through different walls and different doors, continually looping through the arcade, the Chik-O-Fill kitchen, and my apartment. I reached down to the floor of the GameStation at some point and noticed that my feet didn't quite touch it. I pushed my hands through the fake linoleum squares and descended into the Chik-O-Fill kitchen via the ceiling lights.

It was then that I noticed a shadowy figure slumped in the far corner near the deep fryer. He was transparent and shimmery, like me, and also sort of melted-looking. He seemed to be watching me.

"Hey," I said.

"Hey," he responded.

"Umm, do you know what's going on here?" I asked, since he didn't seem very talkative.

"Yeah," he replied. "We're ghosts, duh. How many places did you get?"

"Uhhh . . . three, I think? I keep going from here to the GameStation across the mall to my apartment. But what do you mean, we're ghosts?"

"Just what I said," the figure by the fryer answered. "I died here several years ago after a deep fat fryer accident melted my polyester uniform onto my skin. Then a couple of seconds later, here I was. And here I am."

Whoa! I had heard that story!

"No way . . . you're George Jaffer? Wow. They still talk about you here." I wasn't quite sure whether to tell him it was nice to meet him or say I was sorry about what happened to him, so I changed the subject. "Umm, I'm O'Wayne Alger."

"Yeah, I know," said George Jaffer's ghost. "I've been watching you since you started to work here. I didn't know you'd died, but I'm not surprised to see you here since you did. I figured this would be one of your places, since you didn't seem the sort to have a lot of other ones."

George's ghost slumped shimmering, silently.

"So, uhh, how many places do you have?" I asked, trying to keep the conversation going.

"Also three," said George's ghost. "That's pretty common. I've never met another ghost with more than four, and only a couple with just two. They usually give you your home and your work and maybe one or two other special places for you. Most of us stop going back to our homes, though, once new people move in or they sell your stuff or whatever. It never really seems like the place where we're supposed to be, and you end up watching your parents or your sister or a bunch of strangers, if they move or whatever, and that's kind of depressing."

As George talked, I couldn't help but notice the obvious damage the deep fryer had done to whatever remained of him, and that got me wondering what I looked like.

"Uhhh, I don't mean to be offensive," I stammered. "But if you're a ghost, how come it looks like you're still sort of, ummm, messed up from how you died?"

"That's how it works," George replied. "You're pretty messed up looking yourself. I'm guessing you got snuffed in a car accident. Fortunately, we don't cast reflections in mirrors, so there's not really any way for us to see how bad we look. But when we become ghosts at the moment we die, that's apparently the form we're stuck with. I've met some ghosts who were disconnected body parts moving about like gross little constellations of see-through meat. I think it makes it harder for them to do what they need to do."

"We need to do something? What?

"That's for you to figure out," George said. "Or not, as the case might be. As best I can figure, we become ghosts because we have unfinished business. And once we finish it, then we can move on, though I'm not really sure where. Heaven? Hell? Eternal rest? Dunno. Nobody ever comes back from there and reports to the ghosts, just as ghosts can't come back and report to the living. But wherever we end up in the end, the problem for right now is that nobody tells us what it is that we have to do, so some ghosts appear and get it right and move on quickly, and some have been around for centuries, in living-people time. I think some of them just stop trying, eventually."

George's melted form rose and shuffled across the room toward me. He reached a stump out and pushed it at my squished left hand.

"Did you feel that?" he asked.

"Barely," I answered. "A little electrical current feeling or something. A tingling pressure."

"Yeah, that's about all we've got," George said. "With practice, you can get living people to respond to you that way, guiding them with shocks and surprises and gentle pressures. We're not strong enough to move solid material objects. I think it has something to do with electrical conductance. Some of the older, more experienced ghosts seem to be able to influence lightbulbs and stereos and other electronic equipment. But I've never been able to do that."

"So we have to figure out what it is that we're supposed to do and then use weak powers to manipulate living people to get it done," I said, more statement than question. "Do you have any idea what you're supposed to be doing?"

"I thought maybe it was to save other people from deep fat fryer accidents," George said. "But I've averted a couple of near-disasters — including one where you almost flipped a basket full of battered riblets onto your feet — and I'm still here, so that's probably not it."

"Maybe it's at your other place," I suggested. "Where else do you get to go?"

"Well, my apartment, though I don't go there much anymore, like I said." George paused. "And also the Ladies of the Roadhouse strip club down in Hyde Park. I used to spend a lot of time there. Looking. You know." He paused again. "I'm not sure what else I can do there. Though it's not a bad place to kill the time, as it happens. I can look at the girls from places I didn't used to be able to."

That made a creepy scene even creepier. "Well, uh, I guess if you're here in the Chik-O-Fill a lot, then maybe I'll focus on the GameStation," I said. "Thanks for helping explain things. That was really helpful."

"That's all right," said George. "It always seems like we ghosts overlap this way. I've never heard of a ghost who didn't get an orientation pretty soon after he became . . ."

And then George Jaffer's ghost flickered before me the way an unprotected game console does during a brownout, and he vanished.

Maybe his unfinished business had just been to tell me that I had unfinished business?

Or maybe he just decided he'd rather hang out at the strip club than with me?

Either way, I reached up toward the ceiling and pulled myself through it and onto the floor of my apartment, and then I jumped straight into the front of the refrigerator there and ended up back at the VektorSchift console.

I was pretty sure that if I had unfinished business, this was where it was.

ଓଓଓଓଓ

Things were quiet and subdued at the Quemby Mall GameStation for a few weeks after O'Wayne Alger's cremation. While some folks thought the best way to celebrate O'Wayne's life and work was to continue the struggle to complete level one hundred on the VektorSchift console, others felt that it was disrespectful to replace any of the ten "OWA" scores on the "Superior VektorSchift Warriors" screen, and if you couldn't excel, then what was the point of playing?

After what was deemed a respectful interlude, Roger Evers decided that the only way to get the quarters flowing again was to eliminate O'Wayne's presence in the arcade, giving new VektorSchift players a tabula rasa for their own successful campaigns. He pulled the machine away from the wall after work one night and reached for the reset button, but just as he was about to press it, he felt a sharp electrical shock in his wrist. He recoiled and stared at the power cord to see if it was properly insulated and plugged in.

It was, so there was no obvious ground fault potential to shock players or scramble the machine's processor, either of which would have been bad for business.

He reached for the reset button again and felt the same sharp shock, then a third time. At which point he laughed a nervous little laugh and pushed the machine back against the wall, but not before toggling the payment method switch from quarters to tokens. If he couldn't reset the damn thing, at least he could create an incentive to play it by selling tokens two-for-one for a few weeks. He figured the gamers' frugality would overcome their aversion to playing a dead man's game, eventually.

And he was right. Within a few weeks, traffic at the VektorSchift machine was robust, and a few weeks later still, two players had emerged as arcade favorites to supplant O'Wayne Alger as the most superior VektorSchift warriors at the Quemby Mall GameStation.

Ricky Wolstenholme was a rich kid who lived near the country club. He was football-player fit and popular in his school, and he often brought his girlfriend (cheerleader) with him to sit on a stool and watch him play. (Roger Evers saw so few girls in the arcade that he opted not to enforce the "play to stay" rule in her case.) Ricky was dismissive of the arcade's clientele, for the most part, except for when he was having a strong game, at which point he'd whoop and yell to make sure that he had an audience around him (and his girl).

Balasz "Barney" Bartok was cut from something more akin to O'Wayne's musty cloth. His family had moved to Quemby from Hungary two years earlier, and his English was still weak. He dressed in what were clearly hand-me-downs or Goodwill relics, with nothing quite fitting, or matching, or adhering to current local fashion, even at the GameStation. He was studious, though, and he brought a quiet intensity to the VektorSchift console whenever he could angle his way in between Ricky's seemingly endless streams of quarters, earned caddying for his dad's business partners.

Barney was the first of the two contenders to finally knock one of the "OWA" scores off the "Superior VektorSchift Warriors" screen, earning the number-ten spot (credited to "BAR") with a striking level ninety-four performance, rich with valuable bonus heptaparaparshinokh points. But Ricky soon caught and passed him, scoring the number-eight spot (credited to "RCH") when he broke level ninety-five for the first time.

The pair slugged it out for a couple of months, trading improved scores until only the top three spots still bore the legendary "OWA" tag, with "RCH" and "BAR" sharing the leader boards' lower registers. Ricky grew openly and vocally hostile and abusive toward Barney around this time and often shouted or made sudden movements behind the Hungarian youth when he was engaged in particularly strenuous combat or navigation situations.

Despite the distractions, Barney again took the lead and became the first of two warriors to break onto level ninety-eight, capturing the number-three spot for "BAR." As he grinned sheepishly after entering his personal code onto the "Superior VektorSchift Warriors" screen, Ricky knocked him off the stool, gave him a blisteringly tight wedgie, and taunted, "Who's superior now, bitch?" as the smaller boy cowered. Roger Evers had to issue Ricky an Arcade Red Card, with its attendant one-day suspension. The crowd would have booed, if they hadn't feared similar mistreatment.

When Ricky returned two days later, he sat down at the console, girlfriend at his side, two thick rolls of quarters clutched in her tiny, manicured fists like brass knuckles. Ricky played some inspired games that afternoon and in the days that followed, but it seemed that every time he got to level ninety-seven, his hands would jerk unexpectedly at odd moments, and he'd drive his Kudusai Klipper smack into a seemingly predictable b'boombot swarm or mistime his periapsic dives and crash into the bibbeblack hole or make some other shocking, unforced error uncharacteristic of his state of his play up to that point. He routinely rose, screamed, cursed, pointed, and blamed the machine after such meltdowns, only quieting down when Roger drifted over with a stack of Arcade Yellow Cards. (No Red Card could be issued without another customer's being touched, alas.)

Try as he might — and he tried often — Ricky could never advance past level ninety-seven. Barney, on the other hand, seemed to improve even more as he got deeper into the game, making seemingly supernatural adjustments and decisions to avoid the dreaded Asbury Pokes and dive successfully into to the tiniest food-ends of the snakiest worm-holes with grace and deftness. As in O'Wayne's days, the arcade's customers began to sense history in the making when Barney played — and flashy, all-hat-no-cattle overcompensation when Ricky sat before the console.

Ricky's time at the arcade diminished when football season began — at least, that's what he told people, since he'd begun to develop a whiff of loserdom among the knowing gamers, a rep for being a choke artist with arguably strong fundamentals who just couldn't seal the deal. This gave Barney more time to play, and the quiet Hungarian capitalized: he broke into level ninety-nine and earned the number-two spot for "BAR" soon thereafter, leaving only a single "OWA" atop the "Superior VektorSchift Warriors" screen.

It was the first Saturday in October when it finally happened. With grace, finesse, discretion, and serenity, Barney Bartok become the first player in known history to penetrate level one hundred on the Quemby Mall GameStation VektorSchift console. It threw some theretofore unseen boss-level adversaries at him (Johnny Too-Bad was a crowd favorite), but it also gave him a surprisingly high quantity of vrooom and groon and Prince Rupert's Fire reserves, so that it was only a matter of minutes before he sailed through the sheltering sky and, at last, landed his Kudusai Klipper on the stylized green-and-blue planet he and every other VektorSchift Warrior had sought all these years.

"EARTHBOUND," said the screen.

And then, "GAME OVER."

And then, "YOU ARE NUMBER 1. ENTER YOUR NAME."

And that was it. The gamers erupted in cheers as the time came for Barney Bartok to enter his "BAR" tag atop the "Superior VektorSchift Warriors" screen with the first-ever level one hundred complete game score.

He jogged the left joystick once and prepared to press the moonchild button to lock in his "B," but before he could do so, his hands shivered and jerked, his left one rapidly smacking the joystick, his right one jerking above the moonchild button that would carve the first initial of his legend onto the screen. Barney's entire body shuddered, and then his right hand smacked down on the button.

The letter "O" appeared on the screen.

A gasp of horror arose from the assembled throngs. You couldn't undo an entered letter. Having triumphed over the game, Barney Bartok had now blown his chance to properly record his achievement.

As the gamers continued to vocalize their dismay at such a beginner's error, Barney Bartok's body and hands continued to shake and shudder, his right hand eventually slapping the console again.

The letters "OW" now appeared on the screen.

"Not cool, dude!" shouted a gamer from the back, and the mood of the crowd moved from dismay on Barney's behalf to a sense of moral outrage. What was this all about? Why would he do such a thing? Was it homage? Or heresy?

Barney, obliviously, continued to shake and shiver, and predictably, seconds later, his right hand slapped the console's moonchild button.

"OWA" was the number-one Superior VektorSchift Warrior of record, now with a perfect level–one hundred score. Balasz "Barney" Bartok's hard work, dedication, and ultimate achievement had vaporized in a confusing moment of derangement or delusion or disrespect, depending on how one looked at it.

No one who witnessed that moment was happy, least of all Barney, who flung himself away from the console as if in pain and lurched out through the flickering neon portal of the Quemby Mall GameStation, never to pass through it again.

Gameplay on the VektorSchift machine petered out almost immediately thereafter. Two weekends after the big night, Roger Evers unplugged the console and prepared to return it to the regional distributor.

He felt no unexpected shock when he did it.

଄଄଄଄଄

I had thought it was hard to make Ricky Wolstenholme mess up every time he got to level ninety-seven, but that was nothing compared to how much effort it took to keep Barney from putting his "BAR" at the top of the leaderboard when he beat level one hundred. But I had to, because he didn't deserve it. In fact, he wouldn't have made it past level five without my help. But I couldn't stand to see that that football douche winning at my game, so I had to pick someone, and Barney seemed like he could use some friends and fans for a while. I get that.

After I got him to slap the final "A" button to register our perfect game as an "OWA" triumph, I let Barney go, and I drifted back a bit to admire my handiwork. But then that little drift turned into an unexpectedly big one, and I was pulled from the arcade into some sort of tunnel that squished me down into a long thin tube of ghost stuff and sucked the stuff away into a winding pipe that seemed to press me along, like a snake eating a mouse, only faster and faster and faster.

Then with a gentle "poop" I decelerated and found myself facing a starfield, with the polyps of a wormhole fluttering around my peripheral vision. I blinked and gasped, and I could actually feel and hear that I had done so.

When I looked down, I realized that I had real, solid hands again, and they were wearing gloves, just like those that the Kudusai Klipper Kaptains wore. Only less pixelated.

I also had a console before me, with the familiar twinjet firing buttons, bilateral navigation joysticks, and moonchild, pussyfoot, sus-tayn-z, and polygroon buttons.

And in front of me, where the grainy, green-hued play screen had once glowed above those controls? Oh, my . . . it was stars on top of stars on top of stars, all the way down to the bottom . . .

On instinct, I pressed the pussyfoot button twice to release a blastic rhino, just as the first of the b'boombots hove into view.

The data report line at the top of the bridge screen read "Level 101."

SWEETMAN

Sweetman smelled.

Bad. Real bad.

He knew it. And everyone who worked with him or went to church with him knew it, too. Strangers didn't know it until they got too close to him, but once they'd sniffed him out, they moved away fast and stayed strangers to him forever.

He lived alone in a two-room cabin just outside Bridgefield. During the week, his friends Del and Dick would come pick him up in their truck to take him to work at Phalmouth Construction's heavy equipment barn on Hilton Head (Sweetman had never gotten a driver's license; he didn't like taking tests). They made him ride in the back of the truck, though, which Del had outfitted with a hardtop cover that kept Sweetman out of the wind and rain, for the most part, but let his stench blow out behind them as they drove him to and from work.

Saturdays, he puttered around his house alone, working in his garden, taking care of his goats, waiting for the delivery man from Hughes Grocery to drop off his staples and pick up the twenty-dollar bill Sweetman left on the porch each week. On Sundays, he walked two miles to Pocotaligo River Baptist Church, where he had his own special seat next to the choir loft, with a little window fan next to it that Preacher Benson had installed.

"For your comfort, Samuel," Preacher Benson had said.

Preacher was the only person who called him "Samuel" anymore. He was just Sweetman to everyone else.

Had been for years. He couldn't even remember who first pinned the nickname on him. Once his own family started calling him that, it didn't really matter anymore.

There was one small benefit to his body odor: he had his own office at Phalmouth Construction, with air conditioning, so he could close his door when he wanted to. It made it easy to sneak a nap in during quiet times, since no one would come in to bother him without knocking loudly on the door and asking him to come out onto the shop floor, where the ventilation was better.

Of course, Mr. Phalmouth never admitted that he'd given Sweetman his own office just because he smelled bad. Mr. Phalmouth said he believed in merit-based rewards, and there was no denying that Sweetman was the greatest heavy equipment mechanic that the company, or any other company in the whole of the Low Country, had ever employed.

"You deserve that office, Sweetman," Mr. Phalmouth had told him, more than once, in front of all the others, even. "You sure have earned it."

Sweetman appreciated that little white lie, although he also knew that he had, indeed, saved Mr. Phalmouth and his sons millions of dollars over the years by keeping their heavy equipment in good order, far longer than the normal life expectancies for such complicated and cranky metal beasts.

Watching Sweetman on the shop floor was like watching a brain surgeon at work. Or a ballet dancer. Or a shaman. Or a conductor. It all depended on the wants and needs of the piece of equipment under his ministrations.

He strode among the backhoes and cold planers like a titan. He tamed the compactors and the feller bunchers, making them purr as he touched them. The forwarders, the harvesters, the knuckleboom loaders, and the motor graders called out to him whenever they returned from a job site, and he was there to bandage their wounds and oil their bearings.

Even the road reclaimers, the pavers, and the soil stabilizers — big, nasty monsters that were known for taking legs, arms, and lives every now and again, just because they could — were like gentle lambs when Sweetman was there to soothe them, running his hands through their engines with his eyes closed, reading their inner secrets like Braille.

Sweetman felt complete and connected when he was working on his beloved machines. Not like when he had to deal with people. He felt awkward and self-conscious whenever situations required him to be near others, fully cognizant of the revulsion they experienced, no matter how hard they tried to hide it from him. He gave Dick, Del, Mr. Phalmouth and Preacher Benson credit for being honest with him about his problem and for making appropriate accommodations, harsh as they'd seemed at first.

As a young mechanic, Sweetman had once believed that most problems had tangible, achievable solutions, so he'd tried all sorts of things to alleviate or eliminate his body odor. He'd taken baths in tomato juice, but Del said that just made him smell like a plate of spoiled spaghetti. He'd rubbed lemon juice all over his body. He'd quit smoking, drinking, and eating things like garlic and onions. He'd tried taking multiple showers each day, followed by liberal dustings and rubbings with talcum powders and deodorants. Nothing worked for long enough to make a difference.

Years before, Sweetman had even gone to see old Dr. Gregorie, who told him he was in fine health and that his body odor must just be some divine mystery beyond the understanding of men. Doc Gregorie asked him if he'd read the Book of Job. Sweetman had. Preacher Benson had recommended it to him.

So Sweetman stank. By himself, most of the time, content to work on his machines in the shop, and resigned to the life of a hermit the rest of the week. It had been at least fifteen years since he'd tried any sort of treatment or remedy for his odor, when one Sunday morning in January, just after church, a little advertisement in the Savannah newspaper caught his eye.

"Now open: Jubal's Healing Shop," the ad said. "Natural cures and remedies. Holistic counseling and therapy for weight loss, smoking cessation, phobias, anxiety, stress, body odor, bad breath, and more. Homeopathic, Eastern and Western techniques. On-site massage therapy. Reiki, healing touch, and past-life regression. You are one call away from a happier, healthier tomorrow."

Sweetman didn't call Jubal's Healing Shop that week. Or the week after. But the advertisement gnawed at him, even while he worked on his machines, keeping him from the focus and peace that his labors usually offered. He fought hard to suppress the faint stirrings of hope that he felt, because they had been dashed by reality so many times before.

He went to the Bridgefield Public Library that Saturday and looked up "homeopathic," a term he'd not heard before. It sounded an awful lot like snake oil and quackery to him, and some of the "Eastern techniques" he read about seemed to be part and parcel with cult-like things from which good and faithful Christian men should steer well clear. But then he looked up from his book and noticed two small children with their mother leaving the table next to his to move across the room, the looks on their faces all too familiar to Sweetman, even as the mother shushed her kids from asking the painfully obvious question that intrigued them. Until they were out of earshot, anyway.

That clinched it. Sweetman called Jubal's Monday morning and haltingly explained his situation. The man who answered the phone (it was Jubal himself) had a kind and gentle voice and said he felt confident that he could help Sweetman with his problem. He believed that after a mere two weeks of concentrated holistic therapy, Sweetman would be able to sit where he wanted, when he wanted, with strangers even, without offending a single sensibility. The flutter of hope grew stronger in Sweetman's breast.

The therapy wouldn't be cheap, there was no doubt about that. But Sweetman didn't spend much money beyond the bare essentials, so there was enough in his savings account to take care of it. He couldn't think of anything better to spend his money on, and he didn't have anyone to leave it to, so it didn't make sense for him to die with cash in the bank, and he wasn't ready to give it all to Pocotaligo River Baptist Church just yet.

Work at the shop was usually slow during the short winter season, so Sweetman asked Mr. Phalmouth if he could take a two-week vacation to tend to some personal matters. His boss graciously granted him the time off, with mild noises of concern, as this was the first vacation Sweetman had taken since his mother had died five years earlier. Sweetman assured Mr. Phalmouth that everything was fine and that when he returned, he'd be a better mechanic and employee than ever. Mr. Phalmouth laughed and said he didn't see how that was possible. He was a nice man that way.

Sweetman made a reservation at a small roadside motel a few blocks from Jubal's, and on the scheduled day he called for a cab to take him from Bridgefield to Savannah. At first, he felt like a famous actor, or the president, when the taxi drove up to his cabin to pick him up, but then he caught sight of the driver's face a few miles into their trip and remembered exactly who he was. He rolled down the windows, even though it was chilly out. He didn't look at the driver again until it was time to pay.

Sweetman was surprised (and a bit amused) to discover that Jubal was a heavily-tattooed young man with long plaited braids, piercings in places that looked painful, strings of crystals around his neck, and rows of jangly silver and turquoise bracelets on each wrist and ankle. He greeted Sweetman warmly when he arrived, deftly hiding his olfactory discomfort, but then immediately had his new patient strip down and jump into a hot bath of some sort of liquid wax that smelled like Christmas trees. When Sweetman emerged from the tub, he was given a loose-fitting cotton robe: his uniform for the next two weeks while at the Healing Center.

At the end of the first day (filled with other soakings, drinkings, meditations, dietary discussions, and rubbings), Jubal handed him five brand-new pairs of cotton trousers and five baggy cotton shirts, with socks and sandals to match. The new clothes were included in the price of the therapy, Jubal told him, and the old polyester-blend garments he'd worn to Savannah had been put out in the trash that very day. Sweetman was told to replace all of his other old clothes with similar loose-fitting, comfortable items after he'd completed his therapy. Natural fibers only. His body needed to breathe. Jubal said he would be happy to sell him such extra outfits, if Sweetman wanted them. Sweetman said he'd see.

Over the course of the next two weeks, Sweetman was trained in all sorts of natural remedies for body odor, some ingested, some bathed in, some rubbed on after the bath. There were chlorophyll and magnesium. Zinc and PABA. Witch hazel, alum, and apple cider vinegar. Bauxite, parsley, alfalfa, and radish juice. Rosemary and sage. Turnip juice, wheat grass, tea tree oil, and silicea. Jubal told him he was making great progress. Sweetman had to take his word for it. He couldn't smell anything but that Christmas tree smell most of the time.

At the end of the treatment, Jubal gave Sweetman several bags of pills, salves, and oils, also included in the price of the therapy. When the final bill was presented, it was a good deal higher than Jubal's original estimates. But Sweetman figured he had been a tough case, and he'd gotten all those new clothes, after all, so he wrote Jubal a check in the full amount, without argument or debate. The young man hugged him as he took his payment for services offered. That was a good sign, thought Sweetman.

As was the cab ride back to Bridgefield. Sweetman got in the back of the taxi, left the windows closed tight, and watched the driver. No reaction. No response. Sweetman nearly wept with joy and relief. He hadn't wasted his money. He was cured!

Monday morning arrived, and Del and Dick drove up to take Sweetman to work. He had planned a surprise for them: When the truck stopped, instead of climbing in the back, Sweetman opened the door of the cab and squeezed right in with his friends. They began to protest and to cover their noses and ask him what the hell he thought he was doing, until they realized that nothing was actually bothering them, other than the discomfort of three big men sitting in a seat made for two.

"Well, I'll be damned," said Del. "You ain't sweet no more, Sweetman!"

The three of them laughed and joked all the way to work, cramped up together in the cab of the truck as Sweetman told them of his amazing cure. When they got to the shop, Dick called all the other fellows out to the floor and asked them to figure out what was missing. It didn't take long, as Sweetman stood in the middle of them all, beaming from ear to ear, his distinctive aroma no longer overpowering the smell of diesel fuel and grease.

Mr. Phalmouth slapped Sweetman on the back and said "Well, you are new and improved after all, aren't you? Guess I'm gonna have to think about that private office of yours now, huh? I think Dick and Del might like to have some air conditioning, too."

"So what do we call you now, Sweetman?" one of Mr. Phalmouth's sons asked with a smirk. "Do you want us to check with payroll and find out your real name, or do you remember it yourself?"

"It's Samuel," Sweetman said. "My name is Samuel. Samuel Smoaks."

"Well, all right then, Samuel Smoaks, we got a bunch of big sick machines here that need some love from you after your nice spa vacation," said Mr. Phalmouth. "Can you hear them calling you?"

Samuel Smoaks listened closely and realized with a dawning horror and a terrible ache in his heart that, no, he could not hear his machines calling him, not one word.

They only spoke to Sweetman.

THE RESEARCH ASSISTANT

Dr. Aushan Helling proudly embraced his reputation as a crackpot.

"Ninety percent of all fundamental research must fail if the other 10 percent is to be truly meaningful and transformative," the doctor declaimed to his research assistant, Candona Senver, as they walked together through his jumbled laboratory. "Research projects with a high likelihood of success are just as likely to produce boring reaffirmations of known facts rather than pioneering insights into deeper truths. It's better to waste money than to waste time in a laboratory, since there's always more of the former, while the latter is always running out for all of us. Anyone who thinks otherwise is a fool, and you must develop a thick skin against that type of researcher, along with the bean counters and administrators who always follow in their wake, wagging tongues and fingers."

Candona Senver nodded silently, her eyes warily scanning the piles of equipment they passed as she followed Dr. Helling through his messy scientific domain. The doctor was a zoologist by training and degree, though he had spent his past two post-tenure decades engaged in an increasingly arcane potpourri of cross-disciplinary experiments, the mixed detritus of which spilled from every flat surface in his laboratory. The blend of aging organic, biological, electrical, chemical, and industrial supplies in the lab produced a distinctively greasy aroma that clung to one's clothing and hair, leading students (and some faculty) to snidely refer to

"Dr. Smelling" when discussing his legendarily messy spaces and the long litany of sometimes laughable reports documenting his latest scientific failures.

"The slings and arrows of the unimaginative academic caste mean nothing to me," Dr. Helling continued. "No, I correct that statement: They actually give me strength, because they tell me that I am exploring in spaces where the timid will never venture and blazing paths that are not defined by the rigid lines of a general ledger. Every failure is a success if we learn something from it, while every success is a failure if it does not enhance our knowledge or increase our discernment. The world does not change as a result of confirmatory probings designed to catalog and codify that which is known or suspected. It only changes through true exploration, and that, by definition, requires us to venture into uncharted spaces, where we may frequently get lost and sometimes die. I always aim for those terrifying spaces, and damn the rules, conventions, practices, and prohibitions of the safe and comfortable world around them. This is the truest nature of deep scientific inquiry, and those who decry such an approach are little better than the maze-running rats or light-seeking *Planaria* or sugar-starved fruit flies upon which they so often conduct their boring little experiments."

Candona and the doctor had reached the far end of a laboratory aisle by this point, requiring them to squeeze between the pockmarked marble tabletop and the windowless wall, the paint of which was rubbed off at Helling's shoulder and buttock height by years and years of similar tight passage. On the far side of the table, an algae-smeared aquarium housed half a dozen sluggish fish, clustered glumly at the surface beneath the thin discharge of the circulating filter, hungry for oxygen in their stagnant, plate-glass pond.

"While many scientists hide their failures, I'm proud to document and share mine for posterity's sake," Dr. Helling continued as he ambled down the next laboratory aisle. "Leonardo envisioned helicopters and parachutes, though it took hundreds of years before technology advanced to support his visions. Likewise with Charles Babbage and his analytical engine, or Heron of Greece's plans to harness steam power decades before the birth of Christ. The records of their failures inspired the scientists who followed them, and they undoubtedly reduced the time necessary to bring them to fruition. So I don't give a fig about contemporary peer-reviewed journals or the number of cites I receive when I document my activities, but rather am seeking to create a written record that will outlive us all, providing a road map for the generations who follow, inspiring them to . . ."

Dr. Helling stopped abruptly as he realized that he was walking alone and talking to himself. Turning back, he saw Candona Senver poised at the far end of the laboratory aisle in front of the dingy aquarium, one hand raised above it, her body trembling with tension, faint vocalizations escaping from her mouth as her lips twitched. As he watched, Candona's hand shot into the brackish pool, flipping one of the fish into the air, where it gulped in surprise and writhed desperately before dropping out of sight behind a radiator register. Candona Senver paused briefly, then turned back toward the tank, hand raised for another strike.

With a sigh, Dr. Helling walked back toward his research assistant. Moving up behind her, he shoved his hand sharply beneath her hair, probing the space behind her right ear, eventually finding the location he sought. Candona froze, hand still raised above the aquarium. The doctor then lifted the tail of Candona's lab coat, flipping it over her head. With two hands, he rucked her woolen sweater up around her ribs, exposing the latched compartment in the small of her back. Flipping the toggles on three of its sides, he opened the hinged plastic door, inserted his hands, and gently withdrew a small, orange tabby cat wearing an electrode cap, its wires disappearing into Candona's torso.

"I give you opposable thumbs and bipedal locomotion," the doctor said to the cat, "and all you want to do with them is catch fish? Have you no higher motivations or aspirations than that?"

Dr. Helling removed the electrode cap and set the cat on the floor next to the radiator. It arched its back, yawned, and peeked beneath the cast iron unit to see whether the beached fish was accessible there. Failing to spot it, it sat on its haunches, licked its lips, and looked back over its shoulder at the doctor.

"Sorry about that," the cat said. "I might do better if you'd mix my neuro-stimulant enzymes with a bit of Fancy Feast before you put me inside the Candona Senver unit again."

VERONICA BUGDOCTOR

Veronica Bugdoctor. That's what we call her. She cares for the insects that live on our block.

She shuffles around the neighborhood in her dumpy-old-lady dress, with flowers and stains all over it. She scans the neighborhood for all the spiders and beetles and preying mantises. She makes sure they're OK. She picks up wooly bears and worms off the sidewalk and puts them in the grass so they don't get squished. If there's too many beetles in one flower and not enough in another, she'll move them around so they all get their fair share. She puts out pop cans for the yellow jackets, which is nice, because then they don't come after us so much. Kevin is allergic.

Sometimes Veronica Bugdoctor rescues flies from spider webs and sets them free, and sometimes she puts flies into other webs to help the spiders. That's how nature works, you see, so it's natural and that's OK, although we all feel sorry for the flies that have to be the food. There's a beehive in one of her trees, and they really seem to like it that Veronica Bugdoctor doesn't cut her grass, so there's lots of clover flowers for them. If you stand in just the right spot and look up, you can see the honeycombs inside the tree. We sometimes talk about climbing it to see if we can get some of the honey, but then we think that Veronica wouldn't like that, and we don't want to interfere with her work or cause the baby bees to go hungry. Plus, like I said, Kevin is allergic. Also to peanuts.

Ramona thinks that Veronica Bugdoctor has crickets living in her curly, old-lady gray hair, because when you get close to her it sounds like they're singing in there, but I haven't seen them myself, just heard them. Mom says she's from France. Dad says she's simple. She might be both, I guess, since she doesn't talk much or pay people much mind, just shuffles around muttering to herself while she does her bug-doctor work. Mom and Dad both say her house is an eyesore and that her messy yard hurts their proper *T*-values, but none of us really know what they mean by that. It looks fine to us. Sort of natural, and that's OK.

Veronica has curtains in her windows with flowers on them like the ones on her dress, so we don't really know what the Bughouse looks like inside, the way you can see into other people's houses on the block, especially at night. We saw Mrs. Grayson getting undressed one time in the room in her house with the blue sofa and the painting of a big, red flower over the fireplace. Me and Jimmy and Kevin and Dale wanted to watch more, but Ramona said she'd tell on us if we didn't leave right away, so we did, because she's the oldest, and also a girl. I still think about that sometimes.

You know how animals do the mating on television where one gets on top of the other one like going for a ride? Well, bugs do the mating by getting stuck together at their butts, and sometimes they fly around like that. One day we saw Veronica following some dragonflies that had their butts connected all around her yard. Kevin said she was perverted for watching the mating the way, but Jimmy thought that maybe Veronica had helped them to get together like on the television dating shows. Did you notice that mating and dating rhyme with each other? That's funny. I just noticed it myself.

Me and Jimmy and Kevin live on this side of her house (not together, but in different houses, all on this side), and Ramona and Dale live on the other side (they do live together, since they're brother and sister), so we're always cutting through Veronica Bugdoctor's yard when we're going to one place or the other. We see her there in her yard a lot, of course, but also sometimes in other yards. "Hello, Veronica Bugdoctor," we always say, very polite, and she always looks at us and mutters, but she seems to like the nice way we address her. One time Ramona tripped over a root in her front yard and skinned her knees up bad and was crying, and Veronica brought her a pop and stood there and watched her until she was done crying. So that was nice of her. We teased Ramona afterwards that Veronica must have thought she was a bug, and it's a good thing she didn't get fed to the spiders instead.

Since Veronica Bugdoctor is an old lady and all of us are in elementary school (Ramona is in fifth grade, Dale is in third grade, me and Jimmy and Kevin are all in fourth, which is the average of us all), she's been here on the block doing her bug-doctoring for as long as any of us can remember, and probably for even longer. She's just one of the things that make our neighborhood feel like our neighborhood, just like the swings do, or the little alley between Dale and Ramona's house, and the church that you can climb by putting your hands and feet on each side and pressing yourself up, or the paths in the woods between here and school. Those things never change, they're just always there, always the same.

So that's why my ears perked up one night when Dad said he'd seen Veronica Bugdoctor going through our recycling bin and taking a bunch of newspapers and magazines back to her Bughouse. (Even Mom and Dad called her that, but I don't know if they learned it from us or if we learned it from them.) Veronica didn't seem like much of a reader, and she also didn't seem like much of a trash picker (well, I guess her dress looked like it could have been trash-picked), so Dad telling that story seemed like a weird thing to me, and I told Ramona and Dale and Kevin and Jimmy about it, just because it was different. Like a news report. Flash!

A few days later, we were on the swings, and we saw Veronica Bugdoctor coming down the street, and do you know what? She had some newspaper sheets in her hands, and a couple rolled up under her arm, headed back toward her house. We pumped our swings up high and jumped off as far as we could (Jimmy went the farthest), acting like we were just playing and going to get back on the swings, but then we followed Veronica Bugdoctor from a little ways behind, and saw her take the newspapers up the back steps into what looked like a mud room at the back of the house.

Very interesting, we all thought, and then we decided that we'd be spies and keep a very careful eye on Veronica Bugdoctor to crack the case of the stolen recycling bin newspapers. A few days after that, the case expanded when we discovered that Veronica was also behind the case of the stolen trash can magazines, and the case of the stolen cardboard boxes from outside the church office, too. Also the case of the stolen trash that blew up against the fence around the park where the swings were. It was a full crime spree!

The only mystery that remained to be solved was for us to figure out what Veronica Bugdoctor was doing with all of her loot. It took us a few days more to work up the courage, but the next time we saw her return with a hot load (this time it was from the case of the stolen shoe box next to the Dumpster), we waited until she had gone into her mudroom and crept up very, very slowly and quietly to see if we could peek into the Bughouse and see what was going on. There was a little space in the flowery curtains on one of the windows, so Kevin got in close and put his hands on the sill to lift himself up to peek in and give us the report.

A minute later it happened. He threw his hands up and let out a yell and fell backward away from the window. Jimmy and Ramona and Dale took off like lightning grease, and I started to run, too, but then I heard Kevin say, "It stung me!" There'd been a yellow jacket on the windowsill, and it had got Kevin good. And Kevin was allergic.

I ran to try to get Kevin up so we could get him back to his house so his mom could jab him with the EpiPen, but he was already moaning and crying and wheezing, and I couldn't get him to move. I thought about running to his house and then running back, but I didn't know how much time I would have before the EpiPen wouldn't do the job, and I decided that I needed a grownup's help to do the right thing, so I just ran up and banged on Veronica Bugdoctor's back door, and then ran back to Kevin and told him, "Hang in there, buddy!" and, "We'll get through this, pal!" and, "It's only a scratch!" and other things to cheer him up and make him pay attention.

When I looked up the next time, Veronica Bugdoctor was on her way down the back stairs. She walked over to where Kevin was lying on the grass, and she bent down and picked him up, very gently, like she didn't want to hurt her back, or the person she was carrying. She looked at me and muttered something, and then she carried Kevin up the back stairs of the Bughouse.

We walked through the mudroom area and a messy kitchen and into the living room of the Bughouse. There was no furniture in it at all, just piles of shredded newspaper and cardboard and magazines spread from wall to wall to wall, with bigger piles in three of the four corners of the room. Veronica Bugdoctor carried Kevin to the fourth corner, where the pile wasn't so big, and she gently set him down there. He was very pale and moaning a lot.

Veronica stepped back from where Kevin was lying, and then she reached down with both hands and she lifted up her dumpy-old-lady dress with the flowers and stains on it. Underneath the dress, she had six skinny, hairy legs and six little feet, each one wearing a clunky, black, child-size corrective shoe, like the ones Dale had to wear when we were younger because of his club foot.

I didn't start screaming, though, until the jiggly, green eggs began dropping out of her.

DIX AXIOMATA DE AXON ANON

Osgood, Lord Begabine, eleventh in the line of succession to the thrones of the United Kingdom of Great Britain and Ireland and the British Dominions and the Empire of India, discovered his life's calling at the age of nine.

Young Osgood had been dispatched to summer at Osbourne House, the queen's rural retreat on the Isle of Wight, along with a dozen young Hanoverian cousins from across the continent. His parents had hoped that healthy outdoor frolics in Wight's clear air and rambunctious merrymaking with other privileged youngsters might be restorative for their tremulous and sickly only issue.

Osgood did, indeed, get more exercise that summer than was his wont or desire, though most of it involved fleeing a pair of thick German princeling thugs, who found it endlessly amusing to stuff their smaller, weaker cousin into a variety of cabinets, crevices, and containers about the estate.

One dreary afternoon, Osgood was quietly hiding from the dumpling princes in the foot space under a ponderous Louis XIV reading table in the queen's library. He had pulled a selection of books from the shelves to pass the time, including a large, battered copy of *Reginald Throckmorton's Larks, Japes, Adventures, and Poesy* that, judging by its worn and cracked brown cover and many turned-down pages, had been well loved by many children before him.

Holding the book in his lap, Osgood let it fall open randomly to a full-page illustration and was awestruck by the explosion of color: a fabulous, florid, gold-embossed, vermillion-tinted depiction of two great warrior kings, one Asian, one European, crowned and armored, fighting back-to-back with their swords against an mighty army of Sikhs, Moguls, dervishes, yogis, tigers, elephants, crocodiles, snakes, and unspeakable human-animal hybrids, the likes of which Osgood had never imagined.

And that was not all: Behind the battle scene, coconut and date palms and vine-laden tropical hardwoods swayed above distant bustling marketplaces, between which moved carts, heavily loaded with mysterious boxes and bundles, some drawn by camels, some by elephants, some by men. Sari-wrapped women danced with vulgar monkeys around the page's margins, their fingers oddly splayed and postures oddly supple. The whole scene was framed with intricately knotted vines, heavy with exotic fruits, nuts, and spice pods, which attracted iridescent beetles and gaudy birds of paradise in equal number.

And that was still not all: At the bottom right of the page, inside an elaborately scrolled golden box, was this little poem:

Prester John and Chinggis Khaan
arose before the break of dawn
to put their swords and armor on
and sally forth to war.

Chinggis Khaan and Prester John
swept southward out of high Bhutan
to subdue India and Ceylon
and then they fought no more.

Who were these incredible, virile, majestic warrior kings? Presumably Chinggis Khaan was the Asian one, and Prester John the European, though the chiseled, vigorous, hale, inspirational, and handsome visage of the latter bore no resemblance whatsoever to the pudgy, gouty, pasty Hanover royalty of Osgood's acquaintance, much less their swinish spawn.

Osgood felt a small, moist "pop" in his chest, blushed crimson, and was smitten. He swore a silent oath, then and there, to learn everything he could about this Prester John and to live his life henceforth in adulation and emulation of the dashing warrior king. Flush with desire to begin his studies immediately, he scrambled from beneath the desk without first surveying the space about him and rushed straight into the arms of the sausage-eaters, who carried him out to the garden and left him upside-down in an overgrown marble urn they'd found behind the carpenter's shed. Three hours passed before his cries for help were answered.

ଓଓଓଓଓ

Osgood's afternoon in the urn did nothing to dampen his newfound passion for the wisdom of Prester John, and in the months and years of research that followed, he learned that his heroic idol was an early medieval Christian king of India, directly descended from the Magi, the patriarch and protector of an ancient church founded by St. Thomas the Apostle. While Osgood could find no proof that Prester John and Genghis Khan had actually met and formed an alliance to conquer all of India, he also found no evidence to the contrary, so he accorded Reginald Throckmorton the benefit of the doubt on that particular historical point.

Prester John's splendid kingdom had been home to many marvels, including the true Fountain of Youth (hence Prester John's extraordinarily long and active presence in the world's affairs), while his palace overlooked the very earthly paradise from which Adam and Eve had been ejected. These and other wonders were recorded most explicitly in the "Letter of Prester John," an epistle written by the great king himself to the Byzantine emperor, which circulated widely and in many editions throughout Europe beginning around anno Domini 1165.

Prester John's letter was, at its heart, an open invitation from a benevolent king, seeking kinship with his fellow Christians in Europe and imploring them to follow the route of his brave couriers back eastward into India, thereby joining the sundered branches of the great mother church. The wonders recorded therein served primarily to sweeten the invitation, making it impossible for ambitious adventurers and their patrons to resist its call. In that regard, Prester John more than achieved his goals, as in the centuries that followed, the search for his kingdom provided one of the most significant catalysts for mobilizing European exploration into, and commercial engagement with, South and Southeast Asia.

Unfortunately, for some four hundred years before Osgood's epiphany, Prester John and his letter had also been widely considered by educated men to be a myth, a legend, a hoax, or all of the above. The facts at hand certainly seemed to support such a conclusion: when Dutch and British explorers (first) and colonists (later) brought the Indian subcontinent and Malaysian archipelago into the arms of the European Empires, piece by piece, they found nary a trace of any fabulous Christian kingdom, lost or extant, in the process.

Osgood, who became Lord Begabine at age twenty-two when his father succumbed to his chronic catarrh, did not allow this lack of corroborating evidence, nor the growing bemusement of his family and colleagues, to shake his ever-deepening commitment to his life's great, burning intellectual mission. Based on the evidence of his own research, he believed absolutely that many European explorers had, in fact, found Prester John's kingdom during its heyday from the twelfth to the seventeenth century, but that the successful adventurers were the ones who simply did not return home to their native lands. Why would they? What allure could rotten, medieval Western Europe possibly retain for those who had braved years of travel to reach the very gates of earthly paradise?

It was the losers, quitters, and failures who had framed the modern understanding of Prester John, and the obvious, transparent sourness of their grapes always made Osgood purse his lips in disapproval. It was clear to Osgood that these shallow charlatans had debunked the historical reality of Prester John for no other reason than to mask and deflect attention from their own shortcomings. But Osgood knew that the best-outfitted, best-financed, best-organized expeditions were almost always the ones that never returned to Europe to report on their findings, choosing to bask in glory for the remainder of their days, a fair reward for their valiant efforts. What other explanation could possibly explain the historical anomaly of their disappearance?

At the age of twenty-four, already weary from representing the Crown at various third-tier marching parades and charitable galas as the eleventh in the line of succession to the throne, and temperamentally unsuited for the spoiled debauchery of Edwardian London society, Osgood requested, and received, a Foreign Office posting in Pondicherry, India. He was finally ready to begin his life's work: the quest, on the ground, for proof that Prester John had been a real historic figure, not the result of some medieval fantasia.

ଓଓଓଓଓ

For nearly twenty years, Osgood, Lord Begabine, and his trusted major-domo and manservant, Likhul Bis, had traveled extensively and expansively around British India, representing the Crown in official Foreign Office business, evangelizing the natives into the arms of the Anglican Church when the opportunity presented itself, and searching, ever searching, for traces of the elusive Prester John.

Osgood had concluded early on that it was fruitless to conduct any sort of comprehensive archaeological expedition for ruins of fabulous palaces or fabled cities. Prester John's kingdom had remained isolated from prying eyes when it was vibrant and alive, so it would be orders of magnitude more difficult to locate now, as its remains crumbled into the jungles of Ceylon or sank into the lowlands at the mouths of the Ganges, or were crushed by glaciers inching inexorably out of Kashmir.

Osgood chose, instead, to search for contemporary documentation confirming the veracity of the original twelfth-century "Letter of Prester John." Toward this end, he and Likhul Bis spent a great deal of time during their early years in India conducting investigations in libraries, archives, universities, civic offices, museums, and monasteries throughout the subcontinent, as they followed Foreign Office business from Jodphur to Madras, Karachi to Mandalay, Rangoon to Peshawar, and always, eventually, back to the modest Begabine estate in Pondicherry, where a staff of twenty kept affairs in order while their lord was away.

As years went by and this rigorous academic effort failed to generate any evidence attesting to the existence of Prester John, Osgood decided to supplement his scholarly work with a more anthropological approach, one designed to flush out documents that might be hidden only because their holders had no idea what they signified. So while Osgood focused his efforts within the major Foreign Service Office cities, the faithful Likhul Bis was dispatched on missions up rivers, over passes, through jungles, and across deserts to the most isolated areas of the subcontinent.

Likhul Bis and his team of porters all carried cards upon which were printed the full Latin and Greek alphabets, since Osgood knew that Prester John and his court had been fluent in both of the great Mediterranean languages. In every village and settlement that Osgood's forward exploratory team entered, the natives were offered the printed cards and asked to bring forth any items bearing similar marks.

Most of the items presented to Likhul Bis demonstrated nothing more than the awesome inroads made by the English language into the hinterlands of the British Empire, but occasionally older manuscripts and books emerged, for which Likhul Bis would extend considerate trade terms, returning to Pondicherry to submit the acquired works for Osgood's study. While the anthropological approach did generate some fascinating documents that Osgood dutifully shipped to the Royal Historical Society, none of them provided the empirical evidence he required in order to prove, once and for all, that Prester John had been every bit as real as Osgood himself.

ଔଔଔଔଔ

It had been two days since the normally unflappable Likhul Bis had thundered into the Begabine estate atop his horse, minus his team of porters, a week earlier than expected, shouting "My lord! My lord!" at the top of his lungs, while waving a ledger book above his head.

After his horse had been properly brushed and stabled and Likhul Bis had been afforded the opportunity to bathe and shave and don his dinner attire, the major-domo and his lord sat on the veranda, overlooking the Bay of Bengal, the ledger book between them, as Likhul Bis told the story of his latest expedition.

As Osgood knew, Likhul Bis and his team had been following a barely navigable river deep into the interior of the Princely State of Travancore, northeast of Trivandrum, near the southern tip of the Indian Subcontinent. Eight days into the trip, they entered a small village called Chellanthurithy, and the porters began to pass out the printed cards to the natives, per normal protocol.

A few of the villagers chatted animatedly among themselves for a few moments before gesturing for Likhul Bis to follow them. They wanted to take Likhul Bis to meet a native Javanese man they called Pak Suhud, who had lived in Chellanthurithy for longer than anybody could remember. Pak Suhud spoke many languages, and he had many books. He also knew how to prepare trepang in such a way that it enhanced the village men's sexual prowess, and he was well loved by all in the community as a result. If anyone could help Likhul Bis, it was crafty old Pak Suhud.

Upon reaching the old merchant's doorstep (such as it was, with neither a door nor a step), Likhul Bis presented one of his cards to Pak Suhud, and before he could say a word, the old man's eyes grew wide and he pulled the major-domo into the dark interior of his cluttered home. Carefully opening a carved wooden box, he pulled forth a small stack of unbound parchment sheets and carefully laid them on a table. They were clearly ancient, and they were equally clearly produced by able scribes and illuminators.

Unfortunately, Likhul Bis also noted that they were written in neither the Latin nor the Greek alphabet, but rather in some other ancient alphabet, perhaps Persian or some obscure Brahmic script. As he leaned in to look closer, Pak

Suhud brushed him away and gently lifted the top pages of the stack, leaving a single, final parchment on the table, upon which Likhul Bis saw written, in clear Roman letters, surrounded by a gorgeously painted garland of bay leaves and nutmegs, capped with a European-style crown, the following word:

DIXAXIOMATADEAXONANON

After carefully recording the odd, long word in his ledger book, Likhul Bis asked Pak Suhud what it would cost to acquire the parchments. The old Balinese vigorously declined to sell at any cost, and quickly, but carefully, returned the parchments to their box.

Likhul Bis pressed his case: How had Pak Suhud come by these parchments? Why would he not part with them?

Pak Suhud explained that he had arrived in Chellanthurithy some five decades earlier, long before he had earned the honorific title “Pak,” seeking commercial opportunities in Travancore’s untapped interior markets. Having been raised as part of a merchant family that regularly travelled from Zanzibar to Bali and back, working their way around the Indian Ocean basin, negotiating deals and moving goods between ports as they went, the clever young Suhud had a strong faculty with languages and a hunger for the wisdom of the world’s many learned cultures.

When he arrived in Chellanthurithy, he was taken by the villagers who met him at the river to visit an old, blind Chinese man named Liu Sun who lived in the very house where Pak Suhud and Likhul Bis now sat. Liu Sun was delighted to learn of Suhud's faculty with languages and implored the younger man to read to him from a variety of old Chinese, Balinese, Persian, and other ancient manuscripts that he kept in cabinets, jars, and boxes scattered throughout his home, which he himself, as a young, questing traveler like Suhud, had inherited from an aged Mogul from the far north of India, who had lived there for as long as anybody in the village could remember.

Eager for wisdom, young Suhud obliged Liu Sun, and he marveled at the arcane knowledge contained in the lost manuscripts of Chellanthurithy. In the weeks ahead, Liu Sun confessed that, with no issue of his own, he was now desperate to bestow the inherited library and home to a learned man, like young Suhud, who might keep it and its contents intact for future generations. When Liu Sun died eight months later, Suhud humbly abandoned his prior life and became the keeper of Chellanthurithy's ancient collection of codices, and the villagers soon came to accord him the same deference and charity they had offered to Liu Sun and his long-forgotten Mogul predecessor.

Likhul Bis gently inquired as to whether Pak Suhud knew, precisely, what was written on the parchments containing the odd Roman word. The old Balinese did indeed know: The parchments described a ritual of summoning which, if performed correctly, would result in the awakening of a great and powerful ruler of old, a king who had been sleeping beneath Chellanthurithy for ages and ages and ages. Unfortunately, Pak Suhud noted, shaking his head, in order for the sleeper to be roused, the parchments' instructions required the word of awakening to be read during the ritual by a chaste and priestly Christian man of noble birth, a peer, as it were, to the sleeping king. No one of such a description had ever visited Chellanthurithy in recorded memory, and so the ancient one slept on.

Likhul Bis rode for Pondicherry within the hour.

ଔଔଔଔଔ

Osgood, Lord Begabine, was flummoxed.

Likhul Bis was as dependable a manservant as any lord could ever desire, but the story of Pak Suhud and the sleeping king in Chellanthurithy seemed so outrageous that even Osgood, who wanted to believe in Prester John more than anyone else then living, struggled to accept the tale. He worried, sometimes, that the various bouts of malaria that Likhul Bis had endured over the years might have finally caught up with his poor, hardworking major-domo.

But then, other times, he worried even more that both Likhul Bis and Pak Suhud had spoken the full and accurate truth, and that his entire life, since that fateful summer at Osbourne House on the Isle of Wight, had been guided by divine providence to bring him, Osgood, the fantastically unlikely celibate grandson of kings, to Chellanthurithy, to prove Prester John's existence to the world by awakening him from his slumber.

Osgood would have felt better about following Likhul Bis back to Chellanthurithy had the letters in the parchment actually contained a meaningful, translatable Latin phrase, such as, "Osgood, Lord Begabine, you are summoned by

Prester John." That would have eliminated any ambiguity in the situation, certainly, though it wouldn't have required much of a demonstration of faith.

But the best that Osgood could do as he tried to understand the letters was to break the string into a series of smaller words, all of which at least had some possible grounding in the classical languages:

DIX AXIOMATA DE AXON ANON

Dix was French, for "ten," as any educated seven-year-old knew.

Axiomata was Latin, the plural of "axiom," a statement of fact, the foundation of a proof.

De in various forms was common throughout the Romance languages, meaning "of" or "from."

Axon was Greek, meaning "axis" or "axle" or sometimes, in biology, "vertebra."

"Anon," meaning "coming soon," was anomalous, a word from Old English, not from the Mediterranean basin. This led Osgood to wonder whether it might instead be shorthand for *anonymus*, which was, in fact, a Latin word borrowed from Greek, meaning "nameless."

Put that all together and what do you get? "Ten facts from the unknown axis?" "Ten statements of the imminent axle?" What could either of those possibly mean?

Osgood sighed. He knew, ultimately, that there was only one way to find out.

ଓଓଓଓଓ

Pak Suhud had been elated when Likhul Bis returned to Chellanthurithy months later with Osgood, Lord Begabine, in tow. The old Balinese man clapped with delight when Likhul Bis explained that Osgood was eleventh in the line of succession to the throne of India itself, not to mention the United Kingdom and the various other British Dominions, clearly establishing his nobility. Pak Suhud chortled when Osgood's lifelong celibacy was delicately noted, along with a lengthy explanation about how being so busy with work and the quest for Prester John and various other such time-consuming matters had kept any prospective Lady Begabines at bay, thus far.

His credentials thus established, Osgood was also allowed to view the single Roman-lettered word of incantation at the end of a dense web of elaborate curlicue alphabets, surrounded by faded gold and vermillion illustrations of jungles and animals and fruits and insects and vines, just as they'd appeared in *Reginald Throckmorton's Larks, Japes, Adventures, and Poesy* all those years ago. In notable contrast to the children's book, however, the lascivious dancing women depicted on the parchments were not wearing their saris, and the monkeys with whom they danced were in states of admirable tumescence, which made Osgood blush and turn away.

Pak Suhud said he needed two days to gather all of the elements required to perform the ritual of awakening, leaving Osgood and Likhul Bis and their porters to explore

Chellanthurithy and its environs. They pushed into the forest on elephants, and Osgood was delighted to find a crumbling stone ziggurat at the center of a ring of standing stones, on a hill looking down into Chellanthurithy's valley. Did Prester John sleep beneath this cairn? Or was this just another absurd coincidence in a more and more improbable series of them?

With slowly increasing certainty, Osgood was beginning to embrace the idea that Chellanthurithy might be the gateway to his destiny, the place where all his hard, long work would finally be rewarded, so that he would never again have to see that damnable look of smug amusement that appeared so often in people's eyes when he spoke to them. That would be glorious, as would be the heretofore unimaginable opportunity to bow before the only king who had ever moved him, heart and soul.

☙☙☙☙☙

Osgood, Lord Begabine, was struck by some of the similarities between the ritual of awakening and a proper Catholic Mass, if that Mass had been filtered through five hundred years' worth of Indian cultural sensibilities and was attended by only three people.

Osgood had requested that the villagers and porters not be invited to view or even alerted to the awakening ceremony. If Prester John was successfully roused, they'd know it soon enough thereafter, and if nothing came of the ceremony, then Osgood wouldn't have to endure the guffaws of his porters on the long, slow, disappointing trip back to Pondicherry. Likhul

Bis would be the only witness to the rite in which Pak Suhud and Osgood had speaking roles. He knew how to hold his tongue.

The rite was to be performed just as the sun set, in a forest glade with a brook running down its middle like an aisle between pews, cascading into a sweet, clear pond behind a pair of tables that Pak Suhud had set up to hold the parchments, one with his pile on it, one with Osgood's single sheet. There were candles to be lit, a lamb to be sacrificed, frankincense and myrrh to be burned and waved about, Indian flatbreads and wine to be shared among the three men, and many, many words to be read by Pak Suhud.

Osgood was surprisingly calm as he watched and listened to Pak Suhud reading the ancient texts, mumbling in a language unfamiliar, his fingers tracing the lines across the parchments, right to left, right to left, right to left. As Pak Suhud drew near to the bottom of the penultimate parchment, he gathered all of the elements used in the rite, solemnly carried them down to the pool of water, waded out waist deep and released them.

Dripping incense resin and lamb's blood and water, Pak Suhud then slowly returned to his table, turned his rheumy eyes toward Osgood, Lord Begabine, and nodded his head.

Osgood took a deep breath, and slowly intoned, "*Dix . . . axiomata . . . de . . . axon . . . anon.*"

Nothing happened.

Pak Suhud stared at him, making anxious little "go ahead" motions with his hands. Perhaps his guess at how to divide up the syllables was the problem, Osgood thought. He cleared his throat, and read the text again, this time trying to space them out evenly: "*Dix . . . ax . . . i . . . o . . . ma . . . ta . . . de . . . ax . . . on . . . an . . . on . . .*"

Nothing happened.

Pak Suhud's posture visibly crumpled, and he shuffled back toward his precious parchments, rifling through them, trying to figure out what had gone wrong.

Osgood watched him revisit the text, reading with his fingers running along the lines, right to left, right to left, right to left . . .

Right to left!

The spell of summons was written in a language that was read from right to left, not left to right! The Roman letters had been included in the rite, on their own parchment, so that a chaste Christian son of kings could read them phonetically, but they were written by scribes who wrote from right to left! Of course!

Osgood let out a yell of triumph, and the startled Pak Suhud recoiled so vigorously at the sound that he fell to the ground, parchments scattering around him, eyes wide with surprise.

Stepping forward toward the table containing the final sheet of parchment, the priestly, gentle, chaste, faithful, and royal instrument of God's good will raised his arms to his side, and loudly, confidently read the incomprehensible awakening word, phonetically, from right to left: "*Nona! Noxa! Edat! Amo! Ixaxid . . .* "

ঙঙঙঙঙ

Osgood, Lord Begabine, never saw the luminescent, muscular, razor-toothed tentacle that shot out of the still, sweet pond behind him, separated Osgood's head from his torso on first pass, then quickly swept backward and downward to pulp the remainder of Osgood's body into a fine mist of plasma and bone splinters.

Pak Suhud and Likhul Bis did see the tentacle, along with the rising, towering, crowned figure to which it was attached, but they themselves had only a few seconds to live with those terrible visions, so it didn't matter much, in the grand scheme of things.

Prester John had finally been awakened from his long, dark slumber. And this time around, he was going to make it much easier for people to find him.

THE FIRST YEAR IN FIFTY

For the first year in fifty, he hadn't planted a garden, and every time Bill looked out the back window of his cottage, the opportunistic weeds, vines, and grasses of the South Carolina Low Country reminded him of his oversight. But he just hadn't felt up to planting and tending his own tomatoes, peanuts, and squash through this year's humid growing season, and he had figured that he could buy them all at the market in Bridgefield anyway if he wanted to, although he never did.

He didn't seem to want much of anything anymore, when you got right down to it, and he hadn't, really, since his wife Harriet had died, some four years earlier. She'd been five years widowed herself when he met her at Gregorie's Bar and Grill, where he went to drink beer and watch football, and they were married by Preacher Benson at the Baptist church soon afterward, moving into his cottage on the outskirts of Bridgefield and setting up a home together without any fuss or bother from anyone.

Harriet left Bill's life the same way she came into it, simply and suddenly, by just not waking up one morning, slipping away to glory while he slept beside her. He didn't even notice until after he had gotten up and yelled for her several times, to no avail, while cooking their bacon and eggs, which burned in their own grease while he called 911 and talked to the dispatcher, leaving the cottage smelling terrible for a week, at least.

Harriet had been a good woman, and Bill missed her. Not like that first wife he'd had, the one who ran away with their daughter and his money, never even bothering to contact him at all, until the day when she needed his signature on the divorce papers so she could marry some banker from up Charleston way. Bill didn't even say a word when that woman (as he thought of her) showed up at his front door holding a manila folder decorated with colorful tabs. He just signed where the arrows told him to sign, closed the screen door to the front porch where she stood, went out back, and pulled weeds out of his garden, thinking about how good his peanuts were going to be after he picked them, washed them, boiled them in brine, and ate them while watching his game shows.

But he hadn't grown any peanuts this year, or tomatoes, or squash, or anything, although he still watched his game shows most every day, and football, when it was in season. Bill had bought some boiled peanuts while watching a football game at Gregorie's a few weeks back, but the nuts were too small and slimy, not like the peanuts he grew himself. Plus, the folks at Gregorie's didn't put the right amount of salt in the brine, and the peanuts themselves had a slight tang of vinegar and mold to them that made Bill think they'd been sitting out in the sun too long before they'd been cooked.

He hadn't been back to Gregorie's since then, watching football on his television at home instead, snacking on Vienna sausages and crackers, looking out the window in the back every now and again and shaking his head at how bad his garden looked. Real bad, no two ways around it. Real bad, indeed.

ᏣᏣᏣᏣᏣ

On Tuesdays and Fridays, Bill spent more time looking out his front window than the one in the back, watching for Harriet's daughter Anne, who drove down from Charleston to clean the cottage, wash his clothes, check on his medicine, and bring him groceries or supplies, as necessary. She'd started taking care of those things after Harriet died, and he'd needed the help during those first few months of grief and readjustment, when he couldn't seem to find the energy or organization to feed and bathe himself, much less take care of the cottage and his cats.

By the time he'd gotten to where he could take care of himself, though, he'd decided (without realizing that he'd done so) that he didn't want to bother with those things anymore, and he'd feigned continued helplessness just because he looked forward to Anne's visits. Sometimes he left things out or dirtied dishes on purpose, because he knew that would make Anne stay longer. Bill was willing to put up with her chiding him for his carelessness and clutter while she cleaned, because that was better than not having her there at all.

Thing was, though, the longer he had feigned helplessness, the more helpless he had actually become. And over the course of a couple of years, he stopped needing to dirty the cottage intentionally, because it started happening on its own, without his thinking much about it. It was easier, for instance, to drop peanut shells by his easy chair than to carry them out to the trash on the porch. And it was easier to leave his clothes on the floor by the bed, so he'd know where they were when he got up in the morning. He'd toss a Vienna sausage or two on the kitchen floor when he opened the can so that the cats would have something to eat, rather than fill the bowls on the porch that Anne had set out for their food.

While the cottage deteriorated faster than Anne could keep up with it over the years, Bill had still managed to find the time and energy to keep his garden clean and productive, until this year, that is, when he didn't decide to not plant it so much as he missed the time when he should have done so, without noticing, until it was too late to get it tilled and seeded. He kept telling himself that he'd clean it up and plant next spring, and he told Anne that, too, but neither of them much believed that that was going to happen.

Bill had four acres of land around the cottage, three of them given over to pine, live oak, and Spanish moss, the other one occupied by the garden and a fleet of old cars, tractors, appliances, and parts scavenged from and for them. He'd been a mechanic, years ago, before Harriet even, working on the heavy construction equipment that had been used to build the resorts and golf courses that defined most of the South Carolina coast these days. He came home stained with diesel and grease and went straight to work in the garden, when it was in season, until the rich aroma of the soil and the leaves and the fertilizer drove the smell of the shop out of his sinuses.

A garden was good like that, Bill had often thought, a place where a man could lose himself for a few hours at a time, a place where a man could forget that he had anyplace else to be, ever. Over the course of each growing season, he'd always gotten to know each plant as an individual: what it liked, how it was getting on with its neighbors, how its fruit tasted, which plants were healthy, which ones were not, what was causing them to be sick, and what might make them better.

All told, Bill had always made better friends in his garden than outside of it, with the possible exception of Harriet. Or Anne.

ଓଓଓଓଓ

"So I've been thinking," Anne said, as she folded Bill's shirts and he watched *The Price is Right*, buttering the Hungry Man biscuits Anne had cooked him for lunch.

"Mmm hmm," he said, nodding for her to go on, knowing he didn't need to do so for her to continue.

"I've been thinking that it's getting too hard for you to stay here by yourself," she said. "And it's getting too hard for me to drive an hour each way to come down to make sure that you're getting on OK. And it's getting on close to November, and this place is a nightmare to heat, it's got so many cracks and holes in it, and I don't want you burning yourself up this winter trying to keep yourself warm with that old space heater."

She'd made this point before, and Bill replied as he always did: "I'm doing fine down here, just fine. And this is my home, so where else am I gonna go? A man's gotta have a home, doesn't he?" He paused and thought for a moment.

"Besides, I can buy a new space heater if you think this one's getting too old."

"It doesn't matter if it's a new one or an old one. What matters is that you put it too close to your bed, and you're gonna light your blankets on fire, or your clothes."

"I'll move it, then, if it worries you," Bill said, knowing that he wouldn't. "And besides, where else am I gonna go?"

"You could sell this place and get something nice up in Charleston," Anne suggested.

"Ain't nobody gonna want to buy this old place. It needs too much work."

"Someone might want it for the land. The land is good, if you'd clean all those old cars off of it. And you could rent a nice apartment up in Charleston, and I could come see you every day, instead of twice a week."

"I can't have a garden in an apartment," Bill noted.

"You don't have a garden here, anymore, either," Anne said, pointing out the back window at the weeds.

"But I could have one if I wanted to."

"Do you want to?"

"Yeah, sure, of course I do," Bill answered. "Next year, I'll get it clcaned up and grow some peanuts or something again. I'll definitely do that, next year."

"If you don't burn yourself up this winter."

"I ain't gonna burn myself up this winter. I ain't burned myself up before, so why am I gonna burn myself up now?"

"For the same reason you throw Vienna sausages on the floor now, and you didn't used to," Anne answered.

"Because as much as you don't want to admit it, you're getting older, and I don't think you can take care of yourself here anymore."

"This is my home. This is where I belong," Bill said, pausing before he played the trump card that had stopped this argument so many times before. "And besides, this is the place where your mama lived and where she died. You want me to just sell it and let someone else live here, sleeping in her room, eating in her kitchen?"

Anne stopped her folding and looked up at Bill. He couldn't decide whether she was going to start crying or yelling at him, but he didn't want either thing to happen, so he turned the volume up on the television and looked away, hoping she'd get back to what she'd been working on, or move on to another chore, or find something else to talk about.

"You always say that to me, and I guess I've never been brave enough to tell you that, yes, I do want you to leave this house, absolutely yes, I do," Anne said finally. "This house makes me sad. I've been coming down here twice a week for four years, and I cry just about every time I drive home from here, thinking about Mama and worrying about you. And I haven't wanted to tell you that, because I know it's your home, and I know you want to be here, but I'm just getting tired of the trip, and tired of being sad, and tired of watching you deteriorate here, wondering every time I leave if I'm gonna drive back the next time and find you the same way you found Mama. I can't keep doing it. I just can't. And it's unfair of you to expect me to."

"Then don't come, if it's such a burden," Bill said sharply, hearing his own voice sounding shriller than he could ever remember hearing it sound before. "I don't expect nothin' from you. I don't ask you to come down here. I can take care of myself. You just stay up there in Charleston yourself, and I'll stay here, and I'll be fine. You get on home to the city, and leave me to myself, right here. I ain't no cripple, and I ain't no fool. I can take care of myself, and I don't need you telling me otherwise."

"Then who's gonna tell you that if I don't?" Anne asked, quietly. "Since it's the truth, and someone needs to tell you that. Who's gonna tell you the truth, if not me? And you know that I can't just stop coming down here, because the only thing that would make me sadder than coming to see you would be not coming to see you, although you don't deserve it, most of the time. So who's gonna tell you the truth, Bill, if it isn't me?"

And Bill had no answer to that question, so he turned the volume up on *The Price Is Right* another notch and wondered how that plain, heavyset blonde on the television had managed to get herself a husband without knowing how much a box of macaroni and cheese cost.

ঙঙঙঙঙ

Bill had shot a finishing nail into his hand with a staple gun once, and he'd lost the tip of a finger in a fan belt back when he was a young man, and he couldn't count the number of times that he'd burned himself by touching a part of an engine or exhaust that hadn't cooled properly before he got to working on it, but none of those accidents had ever hurt the way that this one did.

He'd heard one of his cats crying out back and had gone out to see what was bothering her, but she'd scooted under the porch as he came out the back door. Bill had gone over to the far side of the porch, leaning way out to see if he could see the cat, at which point he'd lost his balance and fallen awkwardly off the porch's edge. It was only about four feet down to the ground, but he twisted as he fell, landing on his right side with his arm outstretched beneath him. He felt the shoulder pop from its socket when he tried to catch his falling weight, and then something cracked in his hip when his lower body hit the ground.

Bill lay still for moment, trying to catch his breath and gather his wits. He was hurt, there was no denying that right from the start, but he didn't realize how bad it was until he tried to turn over and stand. His right arm wouldn't work at all, and the sharp, grinding pain in his hip made it clear that he'd broken something during the fall. He rolled carefully onto his back and shifted as best he could to get his weight off the damaged arm and leg, and then the gravity of his situation hit him, along with another wave of pain, and he vomited, turning his head, coughing and spitting to keep from inhaling the contents of his stomach.

He'd never really thought about putting a railing around that back porch he'd built, since it wasn't intended to be a sitting porch as much as a place to store things that were too big to be stored inside the cottage. There was an old icebox up there, for instance, and some tools, and a pump that he'd planned to rebuild so that he could drain the low spot at the back of his property during mosquito season. People had been talking about that West Nile Virus for the past few summers, and he figured that he might want to do something about the bugs, seeing as how he spent so much time outside in the garden, once upon a time.

The steps up from ground level to the house were at the other end of the porch, and he didn't think he could drag himself that far, much less pull himself up the steps and into the kitchen to phone for help. Had he fallen off the front porch, someone driving past might have seen him lying there, maybe, but out back, nobody was going to see him, and nobody was going to hear him, no matter how loudly he might call for help.

He looked to his left, under the porch, and the cat was there, the one who'd been complaining, back up underneath the house, looking out at him. She meowed plaintively, turned her backside to him, raised her tail and stretched, meowed again.

"You in heat, kitty?" he said aloud. "That the problem? Well, I'm afraid I can't help you with that. I'm afraid I got some problems of my own, problems that some old tomcat ain't gonna be able to fix for me."

He closed his eyes and tried to breathe deeply and think clear. What day was it? He had to count back. Anne had been by yesterday, right? Or was it two days ago? Yes, that was it, it was two days ago. She was here on Tuesday. And now it was Thursday, so she'd be back tomorrow, Friday.

It was about five o'clock in the afternoon when he fell, and Anne usually came around ten in the morning or thereabouts, so if he could hold on for — what would that be, sixteen, seventeen hours or so? — then she'd be here, and she'd know what to do. She'd be able to call for help and get him to a hospital, or get an ambulance out to the cottage, whatever she thought was best.

Whatever she thought was best, that's what he'd do. And he cursed out loud at his own stupidity for not doing whatever she had thought was best whenever she'd talked to him about moving up to Charleston. He could be sitting in a warm apartment right now, watching *Wheel of Fortune*, instead of lying here broken in the dirt, between his ill-built porch and his weed-infested garden. He could have gone to bed tonight and planned on getting up tomorrow morning in time to see the reruns of *Jeopardy* that channel 6 aired at nine and nine thirty, instead of dying out here in the cold overnight and leaving a corpse for Anne to find when she came to clean up his mess.

He turned his head to look at his garden plot. The weeds were thick and robust, stronger-looking than anything that he had ever planned to grow in the garden. But then, that was the nature of weeds, wasn't it? To grow strong where they weren't wanted, to fight against the peanuts and the tomatoes and the squash, to choke out the competition, to return again and again, no matter how many times you pulled them up from the roots or twisted their tops off.

He didn't much care for the weeds, but he sure respected their toughness and industry, and sometimes, when his garden was doing well, he'd even leave a particularly interesting-looking weed to grow to maturity, just to see what it would look like, what it might turn out to be, although he always took care to cut those lucky misfits back before they could poison the rest of the garden by releasing seeds that spun, flew, popped, and jumped every which way when you weren't watching them.

There were a few good plants out there in the garden, even now, a few peanuts that he'd left behind to sprout this year, one robust, if frumpy-looking, squash plant that might have produced some good fruit had the slugs not gotten to each blossom as it ripened. Was that a tomato plant on the back side of the garden? He couldn't tell from where he lay, so he closed his eyes and thought about gardens past, and thought about Harriet, and even thought about that woman, who hadn't really been all that bad, back at the beginning, now, had she? He'd give anything to have her stop by right now, that's for sure, or to have her in the house where she could hear if he called her. But it would be even better if Anne were in there, or if she would come by sooner than usual for some reason, a surprise visit, just for him.

And then his thoughts began to wander farther abroad, to places he wasn't sure whether he was remembering or imagining, waves of pain and waves of regret washing over unknown strands in uncharted regions of his mind, until his consciousness began to ebb, even as he looked toward his garden, and he thought, "I'm cold," and he whispered, "Help," and the darkness spread before his still-open eyes.

ଓଓଓଓଓ

"Shhhh . . ."

He realized that he'd been screaming, or crying, or screaming and crying, when he heard the first soft whisper from somewhere off to his right.

"Shhhh . . . ," again, a raspy whisper, or a low rustle, he couldn't tell which, but he quieted and opened his eyes to see if he could tell where the noise was coming from. Above him he saw the stars, but they were blocked by shadows that seemed to be moving somewhere just above the house. What were they? They were too close to be clouds, weren't they? He blinked his eyes and squinted to focus. Too close to be clouds, definitely. Looked like trees, but they couldn't be trees, either, since the edge of the woods was at least fifty yards away, over on the other side of the garden. But they looked like trees, leaning over him, blocking his view of the sky.

And they seemed to be whispering.

Then the rustling grew louder off to his right, and he tried to use his good arm to raise his body a bit to look over into the garden to see what was making such a noise. But he couldn't move his arm, he found, because his arm was bound tight to his side by what felt like a scratchy wool blanket. And he realized that he wasn't cold anymore, because he was wrapped from neck to foot in the same scratchy blanket. Had someone found him? Why had they wrapped him up and just left him there?

As his eyes adjusted to the dark, he became increasingly convinced that those were trees above him. They were trees, absolutely, no doubt about it. Two large pines and half a dozen live oaks, and as he watched, it looked as if they slowly bent lower above him, the Spanish moss hanging from their branches touching the ground around him.

He realized, too, that the ground around him had changed. Where he'd fallen in dirt, he now saw vines, weeds, peanuts, squash, a swath of dirty greenery running from porch to garden. Beneath him as well, cushioning his back from the gravel and sand spurs that filled his yard.

He could feel the plants moving, beneath him, around him, cradling him, wrapping him in their own stems and runners, Spanish moss beneath his head as a pillow, squash leaves keeping him warm, pines standing sentinel watch over him, the Low Country night silent except for the soft sound of the guardian plants, whispering, "Shhhh . . . ," as he lay wrapped in the cocoon of their foliage.

He smiled, and his fingers gently probed the inside of the cocoon with a gardener's expert touch. That was a tomato blossom, wasn't it? And there's a peanut. And a thistle. Pine needles. Sage. He'd forgotten that he'd planted sage, years and years ago. He rubbed their leaves gently, working the soil of off their surfaces, tending them even as they tended him, gardening by night, warm in his own garden's embrace.

ଔଔଔଔଔ

He was cold when Anne found him the next morning, his hands clenched into fists, his right leg and arm cocked at awkward angles from his body. But he was still breathing, and his pulse fluttered faintly beneath her fingers as she probed his neck and tried to rouse him.

She'd ridden with him in the ambulance and sat by his side as the emergency medical team tended to him, running IVs, getting oxygen into him, cutting his clothes away to assess the damage to his broken hip and dislocated shoulder. He'd kept his hands clenched all the while, and she sat at his side and gently massaged his fists until she was able to work them open.

In each, she had found bruised leaves and twigs and pine needles and matted strands of Spanish moss.

ଔଔଔଔଔ

The nursing home wasn't so bad, really.

He'd spent nearly two months in the hospital, first in intensive care, then in the rehabilitation unit, learning how to walk again, gaining strength in his damaged limbs, before moving to Palmetto Grove, where he had a private room with a window and a television. His room looked out over the Cooper River in Charleston, a couple of miles from Anne's house, and she came and saw him every day, sometimes twice. She'd taken his cats, and sometimes she brought one of them by to visit with him, and they all sat and watched game shows together.

Or they gardened. Bill's room was chockablock with pots, each of them filled to capacity with healthy, thriving plants. They kept the rooms greenhouse warm at Palmetto Grove, and the plants loved the morning sun as it rose over the Cooper each day, the shadows of pine and live oak running across the lawn between the river and the nursing home, climbing the walls, then receding as the day moved on.

He'd gone back to the cottage only once since Anne had boarded it up, taking nothing from the house but a picture of Harriet and an old photo of him and that woman, smiling together long, long ago. Harriet's picture hung on the wall over his television, and he put the other photo in his bedside table, taking it out and looking at it every now and again.

He'd spent most of his time out in the garden that day when they'd last visited the cottage. It was browning under the winter sun, but he slowly walked its rows and carefully picked through the soil, looking for seed pods, shoots, sprouts, signs of life. He'd found a small pine sapling at its edge and had carefully dug it up, wrapping it in Spanish moss and placing it in a bucket until he could get it back to Palmetto Grove, where he'd replanted it, along with all of the seeds and plants he'd pulled from the garden itself.

He didn't even know what most of the plants were as they sprouted and grew and seeded and died, and Anne periodically suggested that he replace those old weeds with flowers, or at least something pretty, but Bill just ignored her and tended to the wild things from his garden as lovingly as he'd once tended his squash and tomatoes and peanuts.

A man needed a home, and a man needed a garden, and a man needed friends, and if a man had those things, then a man's life was pretty well complete, wasn't it?

Or at least that's what Bill thought, as the shadows crept back down the lawn toward the Cooper, and as he sat in his chair, cat in his lap, Anne holding one hand, the other hand idly running through the soil at the base of the pine sapling,

Harriet over the television, on which the Wheel of Fortune was spinning, spinning, spinning.

THE GIFT OF THE PERFUMER

I am a modest man, so it is with no small amount of regret and humility that I must introduce myself to you as the greatest perfumer that Judea has ever known. I leave it to you, dear reader, to evaluate my competitors in the hopes that you may prove me wrong and find me arrogant or misguided, though I doubt that you will be able to do so. Facts are facts, even if they are self-congratulatory.

My name is Aabir Ibn Aariz, and I sell my wares in the market at Jericho. While it pains me to say so, we live in terrible times for nasal aesthetes: the cities of Judea and Samaria reek of filth, as scents human, animal, and earthly routinely compete, one with the other, for primacy in a spectrum of sensory vulgarity. The ripe smells of urine and feces, putrid flesh, spoiled vegetables, mildewed thatch, rotten fruit, leprous neighbors, foul water, ghastly fish, unwashed children, and their filthy peasant parents are as ever-present as sunlight and sand in the day-to-day lives of the average Judean, rich or poor.

The poor ones, of course, have no recourse but to wallow like bits of lamb in the rank olfactory stew in which they all eat, pray, sleep, mate, and die. But the rich ones? The rich ones come to see me.

It is delightful to see the looks on their faces when they approach my shop, where the ubiquitous stench of city life is, for the moment, masked by the aromas wafting from my amphorae of resins and oils. And, though once again it pains me to say so, modest man that I am, I offer the most bountiful collection of delightful perfumes culled from the known world and beyond, scents sublime, magical, mystical, sensual, and soothing. I sell cedar and sandalwood resins, ripe patchouli from India, civet musk from Ethiopia, rare and fragrant fluids drawn from the heads of sea monsters, and so many other wonderful perfumes, all guaranteed to subdue the unruly reek that swirls in the airs about us.

I have neighbors who purchase my wares, of course, usually in tiny portions, trading hard-earned bronze and (occasionally) silver coins for brief reprieves from the noxiousness within which they subsist. But I also have my high-end clients, often Roman officials or their local functionaries, who sweep into my shop every so often to haul away full amphorae of fragrances in exchange for my preferred form of payment: soft, supple, sweet gold.

While I am not a venal man, I must confess that I always find the heft of a sack full of gold to be surprisingly satisfying, both while I hold it and while I make plans to use it for future fragrant acquisitions. Sailors, Greeks, and Samaritans will do most anything for gold, a fact which I have often turned to my own advantage in business, asking few questions, telling no tales.

But I digress. Yesterday, on a brisk, early-winter morning, I was delighted by the arrival of a contingent from the court of King Herod, a most favored client who adores my sandalwoods and cedars and musks and ambergris. Herod's retinue came bearing a wonderfully heavy sack of gold, and after the usual haggling over price and quantity, they left with nearly all my higher-end stock, carrying it away to make the king's chambers, halls, and body smell sweeter than sweet through the wintry months ahead, when foul smells are most concentrated by confinement in the cold.

As Herod's functionaries rode away, I jingled the gold coins they left behind, even while wishing that they'd taken more of my frankincense and myrrh. I was a bit overstocked on those more common fragrances, which are processed from the resins of spiny shrubs native to our region. Oh, well, it wouldn't spoil, and perhaps there would be a plague over the winter. Frankincense and myrrh are, of course, my most popular funerary fragrances, uniquely useful for masking the smell of decaying bodies before they can be properly sealed away in tombs. A businessman could hope.

Flush with the fruits of a very successful late-season commercial transaction, I spent the day and evening after Herod's contingent departed by emptying an amphora of my finest Greek wine, perhaps mixing it with less water than was advisable. Signs were seen, songs were sung, succulents were slurped, and sandals were slung aside as I collapsed at evening's end, sated, satisfied, serene.

This morning I awoke, bleary and bloated, and again heard the sound of a large train of camels being kneeled outside of my shop. Had Herod's men returned? Were they unhappy with my wares? Who else could be out there with so many men and so many animals?

I rose quickly, head spinning, wrapped myself in bed linens and sleeping robes, and wobbled outside to assess this unexpected assignation. Imagine my surprise when I saw what appeared to be a large, strange courtly retinue, headed by three magnificently clad men, clearly royal material, ably assisted by a small army of drivers, porters, and other functionaries.

"Hail, fellow, well met," bellowed one of the kingly trio in a voice that made my jawbones hurt. "We are here to see your master, the great perfumer, Aabir Ibn Aariz! Will you bring him to us?"

I pulled my bedclothes about my shoulders, focused my gaze, and tried to rise to a respectfully sober stance. "You have found me, fair traveler!" I shouted back, at an equally absurd volume. "For I am the one you seek, Aabir Ibn Aariz, master perfumer of Jericho! How may I help you and your most sublime and magnificent colleagues?" (I have learned, after many years in business, that a little flattery often goes a long way.)

"Ho ho!" shouted the enthusiastic kingly personage. "I apologize for not recognizing you! I had expected someone slightly more, ahhh, *grand*, given all that we have heard about your talents as a perfumer! But no mind, let us treat! I am Melchior, a king of Persia! And let me introduce you to my companions . . . Caspar of India! And Balthazar of Arabia!"

The two other kingly personages separated themselves from their retinue and stepped forward, nodding respectfully, but in a fashion that made it clear that they were acknowledging someone of lesser stature. They were, indeed, stately individuals, exotic, exquisitely dressed, and apparently eager to trade.

"We have ridden for many weeks out of the East!" shouted Melchior. "Following a star! A star that signifies the birth of a king greater than any of us, and greater than any king who has ruled any kingdom throughout the entire history of humankind! We are certain that you know of whom and what we speak, yes?"

A king? A star? Well . . . I knew nothing of a king, but, yes, I had seen the new, bright light in the sky in recent weeks, though as a learned fellow, I had just assumed that it was a comet. But who was I to argue with a customer?

"Hail Melchior! Hail Caspar! Hail Balthazar!" I shouted, rising to the spirit of the occasion. "I, Aabir Ibn Aariz, look forward to assisting your kingly personages on this most fine and fortunate of mornings in Judea! But would it bother your regal selves if I stepped inside my humble abode to dress properly for such an auspicious visit?"

"No worries, master perfumer," said Balthazar, in a more conversational tone. "We are in a hurry, a mere day or two from our destination, so we forgive you your slovenly appearance and would like to make trade, posthaste. We seek gifts for the new King of Kings born beneath the star we follow, and we know you are the only man in Judea who can help us . . . so please, name your price for three amphorae of your highest-quality cedar, sandalwood, and musk. We plan to honor the newborn king with the gift of these three fine perfumes, so that he may grow to sentience free from the stench of common living and base animal vulgarities."

Cedar? Sandalwood? Musk? I had just emptied my stock of all three of those delights to support Herod's court. But who could have blamed me for doing so? Who would have expected these three kings to arrive at my doorstep, seeking gifts after traveling afar?

I tried to plan my next move while gathering my robe in regal fashion. "With all due respect to my lieges and to the newborn King of Kings, I have no sandalwood, no cedar, and no musk to sell today, but I can offer you two delightful amphorae, one filled with frankincense, and one filled with myrrh, if it please your kingly personages to accept these wonderful substitute products."

"Frankincense? Myrrh? What are those?" said Caspar, a bit more aggressively than was necessary for the first line of a business negotiation. "Do they smell good? Are they as nice as cedar, sandalwood, and musk? We certainly cannot show up to visit the King of Kings with second-rate perfume, can we? And what kind of perfumer are you if you do not have sandalwood, cedar, and musk?"

"I am the greatest perfumer in Judea, Your Highnesses," I quickly replied. "But my products are of such exquisite quality that they sell quickly — to kings, no less, though not, to date, to Kings of Kings. Yesterday morning, I could have loaded all your camels down with sandalwood, cedar, and musk, but I have just made a sizable sale of said substances to a significant client of some renown, so I am short in supply to satisfy such an unexpected sale. But frankincense and myrrh are, truly, worthy substitutes, highly popular among Judean high society, and you will certainly make a most inspiring and memorable impression when you arrive with these powerful fragrances, guaranteed to mask the most forceful of foul vapors."

"Hmmmmm," said Melchior, although it still sounded like shouting when he said it. "Very well, then! We will take your frankincense and myrrh, if they will mask the putrid reek of Judea! But we are three kings, and that is but two gifts!

What else do you have that we might bring to the newborn king? What? Speak up! What?"

What else? Nothing else. My shop was empty. Except . . .

"You highnesses, I have the best gift of all for the third of you to bring to the King of Kings," I declaimed, in my most dulcet and persuasive of tones. "I have gold! It is the softest of metals, but that makes it the most malleable, and the most transferable. If you take gold as your third gift, then your newborn King of Kings can return to visit me in due time, any time, to exchange it for cedar, sandalwood, musk, ambergris, or any other perfume that I may ever stock! The gift of gold is the greatest gift of all, as it bestows upon its recipient the future right to a stench-free Kingdom, whenever or wherever he might like it! I hope this pleases your lieges . . . it is the finest offering I can make after your most noble of journeys, and I shall offer all of my wares at a discounted price accordingly, with all due respect for your tiresome travels!"

And they bought my line! Haggling ensued, of course, but an hour later, I had parted with only modest quantities of my ample stocks of frankincense, myrrh, and gold, while Melchior, Caspar, Balthazar, and their retinue rode away, leaving behind a camel, two goats, a barrel of sweet dates, and a beautiful silk cloak. It wasn't even noon yet, and I'd scored mightily, despite my splitting wine headache.

What an unexpectedly fine morning for Aabir Ibn Aariz!

After the three kings left, I retired to my quarters to clear the remaining cobwebs from my head by eating some bread with *za'atar* and some wonderful dates (from the barrel

I had not owned when I awoke), dressed properly, wrapped myself in my fabulous new kingly cloak, and headed down to the well to slake the thirsts of my new camel and goats.

Of course, on arrival there, I was reminded of exactly why my line of business was so successful: a haggard widow hovered over the sulfurous well, with two sallow, half-dressed children at her heel, while one of the neighborhood lepers rang his bell at the edge of the square, lest any clean individual approach him too closely. They all reeked, to put it bluntly. Flagrantly so.

I bustled loudly up to the well with my livestock, hoping to roust the crone and her foul kin to move away, but they did not step aside. And as I drew upon them, oozing with disapproval, I noticed something unexpected: all three of them had multiple sprigs of *qaysum*, the native lavender cotton of Judea, tucked into the folds of their ragged clothes.

Why would the widow have put them there? To help them cope with the awful stench of existence in Judea, of course, in her own simple way.

The widow and her spawn could never have afforded my fragrant wares, but they responded to the same need that drove me — and the three kings — to seek the small, sweet remedies that make being a smelly living thing in an awful, stinking world ever more slightly tolerable. I made perfume. They picked flowers. Different means, same motive. Though nobody appreciated their efforts but themselves.

Now, I have mentioned before that I am a humble man, but I hope I have also made it clear that I am a pragmatic businessman who minds the bottom line. So I am not normally subject to flights of fancy or fits of largesse. But seeing these people at the well — so far beneath my standing and so beyond the purview of Caspar, Melchior, Balthazar, and their like — striving in their own humble way to achieve the same tiny pleasures that we, the fortunate wealthy, use our riches to pursue . . . well, I was touched, I admit it. Terribly so, though I don't know why this scene moved me so much today, when I had ignored it so many times before.

I had so much to be thankful for, so many comforts and joys, and they had so few, though even the widow and her children could be considered fortunate when one pondered the plight of the bell-ringing leper.

Feeling so unexpectedly moved (and, perhaps, addled by wine), I made what was probably the worst business decision of my life: I tugged my new camel toward the woman, and I handed its lead to her. And then I took my two goats, and I led them toward her children, and I gave their ropes to them, without a word. And then I walked over toward the leper at the edge of the square, who recoiled as I approached him, and I removed my new, kingly silk cloak, and I laid it over his shoulders.

And then I walked away briskly, without ever meeting their gazes, incredulous as I expect they were.

At least I still had that fresh, new barrel of dates when I arrived at home, and I must say, they were sweet indeed.

LISTEN

"I think I need to go to the vet," said Hamburger.

The ponderous gray tabby sat on the kitchen counter next to his human companion, Chloe, watching her attentively as she washed the dishes.

Chloe nodded slightly but didn't respond.

"I said, 'I think I might need to go to the vet'," Hamburger repeated. "This scratch on my head is really starting to hurt. Can you take me to the vet to get something for it, please?"

Chloe turned off the tap water and looked at the cat while drying her hands on her apron. The scratch above his right eye had definitely gotten infected. Could be a hematoma underneath it. Probably would need to be lanced and treated with some antibiotics, if that was the case. She hoped it wasn't.

She sighed. "Serves you right, you know," Chloe said. "If you didn't pick fights with Flyball all the time, she wouldn't have popped you that way."

"I didn't pick anything," Hamburger protested. "Fly popped me for no reason. If I'd been bothering her, I would have been ready when she scratched me. But she just smacked me while I was sitting in the sun, minding my own business. And now it hurts, and I want to go to the vet."

"I don't have any money for the vet right now, Hamburger. Let's put some antibiotic cream on it and then maybe a warm washcloth and see if we can't make the swelling go down."

Hamburger hopped off the counter and headed for the bathroom. "Just make sure you wring the water out of the washcloth before you use it," he said as he left. "You know I hate it when you get me all wet."

ᏳᏳᏳᏳᏳ

It was bedtime, and Chloe hadn't seen Skitsy all day.

"Has anyone seen Skitsy?" she called. "Hamburger? Jeep? Flyball? Sammy? Anybody?"

"Nope."

"Sorry."

"No. Haven't seen her."

"Sammy? Have you seen Skitsy?"

"She was under the trailer before dinner, I think," Sammy murmured from beneath the comforter. "But I haven't seen her since then."

"Hamburger, will you please go check under the trailer and see if Skitsy's there?" Chloe said, nudging the portly tabby with her foot.

"Why do I have to go?" Hamburger groused. "I'm hurt. Make Flyball go."

"No, you go. Skitsy's afraid of Flyball. She only listens to you. Go find her. Quick. Otherwise it'll be your fault if she gets eaten by a snake tonight."

Hamburger waddled to the edge of the bed and jumped down with thump. "I don't care if she gets eaten by a snake," he said. "There'd be more food for the rest of us if she did."

"You don't need any more food, you fat old man," Chloe scolded.

"Don't blame me for being fat," Hamburger said as he squeezed through the cat door. "I didn't go and have *myself* neutered."

ଓଓଓଓଓ

"When are the ladies coming?" asked Skitsy, while washing her tail. "I don't like them."

"Oh, they should be here any time now, I guess," answered Chloe. "But they won't hurt you. I don't know why you're scared of them."

"They don't like the way we live. They don't like our trailer. They want us to move. That's why we're scared of them. This is our home."

"That's right. It is our home. And it doesn't matter what . . ."

Chloe was interrupted by a loud banging and clattering as Hamburger, Jeep, Sammy, and Flyball all tried to get through the cat door at the same time.

"Car!" yelled Jeep.

"The ladies are here!" shouted Sammy.

"Ow! Ow! Why'd you do that, Flyball, I'm just trying to get inside! Ow!"

One by one, the cats funneled in through the door, then skittered across the linoleum floor and headed for the bedroom, where they would hide in the closet until the hated ladies had gone. Skitsy's paranoia was contagious. Even Chloe felt it sometimes.

She took a deep breath, ran her fingers through her hair, checked her clothes for food stains, and smoothed out her shirt as best she could. Then Chloe looked at the red light above the door that would flash and let her know when Norene, her social worker, had pressed the button outside. The button made no sound, which didn't matter, because Chloe couldn't hear it if it did.

The red light flashed, and Chloe peeked through the curtain before opening the door. Norene stood on the porch, scowling, with the county's sign language interpreter standing behind her, her hands at her side, silent. Chloe let them in.

Norene flopped on the couch, fanning herself, while the interpreter sat on Chloe's ottoman. The social worker jumped straight into her usual litany as the interpreter furiously signed to keep up.

"You can't stay here," the interpreter signaled, translating the highlights of Norene's standard monologue. "It isn't safe for a woman to be here alone, especially a woman with your special needs . . . it's not sanitary . . . you need other human contact . . . too many cats in this trailer . . . what about the doctor . . . too much starchy food . . . poor personal grooming . . . no food stamps for cat food . . . something has to change, Chloe, something has to change . . ."

Chloe stopped paying attention to the interpreter after ten minutes or so and nodded at Norene until the social worker stopped, shook a finger Chloe's way, and left in a huff, still fanning herself, sucking the interpreter out in the slipstream of her distaste.

ଓଓଓଓଓ

It took about an hour before the cats felt comfortable enough to emerge from the closet and come sit with Chloe.

"Why do the ladies keep coming and telling you that you have to leave?" asked Flyball. "It just makes me want to scratch the stew out of them both! Haven't you told them a thousand times that you're happy here?"

"Yes," said Chloe, scratching Hamburger's head, which seemed to be healing nicely. "But some people just don't know how to listen."

COKESBURY ROCKS

I suppose I should start this story at its beginning, except that to tell you about the beginning, I probably need to tell you what came before it.

My name is Kenny Broadhead, and I'm from Cokesbury, North Carolina. Well, actually, that's not completely true. I was brought up just down the road from Cokesbury in Chalybeate Springs, but for professional reasons, I've found that it helps to say that I'm from Cokesbury. This is because the folks I work with sometimes are interested in things like cocaine or Coca-Cola or cock-fighting or what have you, so "Cokesbury" adds a little humor and zest to things that way, right off the bat. Plus, a lot of them also have a hard time spelling tricky words like "Chalybeate," so there's that, too.

Now, when I say "professional reasons," what I mean is . . . well, boy, I tell you, it's hard to tell this kind of story to strangers like you, since every piece I tell you about has another piece that comes off from it that you have to understand too. So let me back up a minute to clear up that when I say I claim Cokesbury as my hometown for professional reasons, I don't mean because of my day job, which is working as a bug exterminator for my uncle Dickie Deems' Doornail Dead De-bugging Depot.

The folks I work with at the Doornail Dead De-bugging Depot might or might not be able to spell "Chalybeate," but I don't think they'd hold it for or against me if I was from there or from Cokesbury. When you got bugs, you don't care where the exterminator is from, so long he gets the job done and doesn't mess with your wife or your daughters or your livestock or your crops or your car. Or your dogs. Unless they got bugs in 'em, of course. That changes everything.

No, the professional reasons I'm talking about here with regard to Cokesbury being my hometown have to do with my night job, which is being the lead guitar player and singer of the Burzürkers, North Carolina's Finest Scum Rock Band. There's two *u*'s in "Burzürkers," if you're writing this down, and the second one has those two dots on top of it. Wardrow, my drummer, he thought we should have the dots on both of the *u*'s, but I told him it wouldn't make sense that way, since then one *u* wouldn't sound any different than the other *u*, so we might as well not have any dots at all if that was the case. And you need your dots in the scum rock business, right?

Also, if you're writing this down, then you should put that bit about "North Carolina's Finest Scum Rock Band" with all capital letters at the start of each of the words, since it's a trademark sort of thing, like a title, and not something that somebody elected us to or anything. I've been looking into whether we can put one of those letters in a circle next to it so other scum rock bands in North Carolina can't use it, but I haven't been able to quite get my hands around whether it should be a *C* in the circle or a *R* in the circle or a *TM* in the circle.

Any of you lawyers willing to give me a little help on that one, while we're here, anyway? No? OK, understood. Time and a place for everything and all that.

So anyway, I'm Kenny Broadhead; I'm from Cokesbury, more or less; I'm a bug exterminator by day and a scum rocker by night with the Burzürkers. There's two other fellas in the band too: Wardrow Deems, who I mentioned already, is the drummer, and his brother Delmas Deems is the bass player. Wardrow and Delmas's daddy is Dickie Deems, who owns the Doornail Dead De-bugging Depot, so he's my boss, in my non-Burzürkers job. His sons work for him too. Bug killing runs in the family, I guess you can say.

I mentioned that Dickie's also my uncle, but I hadn't told you yet that he's actually my uncle twice, since Wardrow and Delmas are kin of mine on both sides of the family: our mothers are sisters, and our fathers are first cousins. So I guess that makes me and the Deems boys both first *and* second cousins to each other, right? I never really did figure out that relationship exactly, but since they aren't girls, and they don't have sisters, it never really mattered to me in any important way.

Now, let's see, me and Delmas and Wardrow started playing music together about twenty-five years ago, around the same time that we all first started driving fast cars and smoking tobacco that we stole from curing sheds and shooting turkeys out behind the elementary school and messing around with girls and making moonshine and, you know, all the other sorts of usual things that kids around here get into when they turn twelve or thirteen or so. But the band gave us something to focus on, a dream of something better than what we had, maybe even involving satellite television or a swimming pond without water moccasins in it or a date with one of those girls on Uncle Dickie's tool calendars.

I guess you could say that the band kept us off the street, except that we didn't really have a street so much as we had a dirt road. But that dirt road connected to a street eventually, and we stayed off of it. So we have the band to thank for that, for sure.

So now let's push the fast forward button a little bit, if that's OK. As it turns out, the Burzürkers actually have gotten to have quite a following in a lot of roadhouses and bars around these parts. We're pretty popular with the kinds of ladies that like NASCAR and tattoos and Skoal Bandits and who might go home with you if you buy 'em enough drinks, or who might just take their tube tops off on the dance floor if you don't have quite enough money to get that many drinks into them. And that makes us pretty popular around here with the fellas, too, you know what I'm saying?

So that's all good, but then there's another part about the Burzürkers story too, since we were even a little famous around the rest of the country, for a little while, once upon a time.

Maybe you heard of us back then? No?

Well, let me jog your memory a bit: Do you recall when Missus Pepper Prong, that senator's wife, did those scum rock music investigations up in Washington some years back, after she caught her teenage daughter listening to a dirty record by that skinny little black fella named, uh, Duke, or something like that? Well, after she got done whippin' her kid, I guess, she went and did all sorts of record shopping, and she found all sorts of scum rock bands from all over the country, and she brought them all to Washington to talk about them and play their music for folks, so they could have some talks about what was good music and what was not.

I didn't get to go those meetings up in Washington, since it was in the late spring, and that's peak bug-killing season hereabouts, but I'm honored to say that the Burzürkers got three songs on Missus Pepper Prong's list, out of all of the scum rock bands around the whole country.

Let's see, there was "Bathtub Smack My Bitch Up" first, and then they played "Flush the Fetus," and, uh, the third song was "Shooting Mexicans in a Barrel," if I recall correctly. And if you don't mind me patting myself on the back a little, I'll tell you that I write all of the Burzürkers' songs myself, so that was my work on display up there in Washington, taken right off the cassette tapes I had made to sell at our shows a couple of years earlier. We were the best of the worst, thanks to Missus Pepper Prong, and we got written about in all sorts of newspapers and magazines because of it, all over the country.

You know that guy with the mustache, Frank Zeppelin, or whatever his name was? He was there too, talking to the Congress, and even he admitted that we were "execrable" and that our talent was, uh, "bereft," I think was the word he used. So that's pretty good for a little scum rock band from Cokesbury, right?

Man, I sure was proud to be an American that day, yes sir, when I heard that they had played those songs up there in front of the Congress and everything, let me tell you. I mean, we really were North Carolina's Finest Scum Rock Band that day, even without the *R* or the *C* or the *TM* in the circle after it. So if you're writing this down, then let me just say a big "thank you" to Missus Pepper Prong for being our most famous fan.

Thank you, Missus Pepper Prong! We love you big in Cokesbury! Whooooo!

What's that? Oh, all right, sorry. See what I mean? How can you ever figure out where a story starts, anyway? It ain't like I woke up in the Garden of Eden one day, where everything that happened after I woke up had nothing to do with what happened before. That would make storytelling for strangers easy, since there wouldn't have been any before, before, and you could just start at the beginning. Well, at least there wouldn't be any before, before, that I was aware of, anyway, since I would have just woke up in Eden, on the first day. Though, come to think about, I guess the Lord would have been messing around for a few days before he made Eden, but that would be his before-story, not my before-story. Hmmm.

All right, all right, anyway, I think I'm getting close to the beginning of this here story you want to hear now. So, let's see, you know about me, and you know about the Burzürkers, and you know about Cokesbury, and you know about Missus Pepper Prong. But, uh, now you can forget about Missus Pepper Prong, since she doesn't really have anything to do with this particular story anymore. I just wanted to tell you about her and about when we were famous, and to thank her, in case you're writing all of this down. For the record, as it were.

OK, so this story starts a month or so back, right after Labor Day, when me and Wardrow and Delmas set off to do our fall shopping for the band. Well, we called it "shopping," though I suppose that in the eyes of the law, it might could technically be called "stealing." But I'll call it "shopping" in this story, if you don't mind, since that's how I think about it, and you can just replace that word with "stealing" in your notes there, if you're writing all of this down.

Are you writing all of this down? Yeah? And recording it? OK. I thought you might be. Just checking. I mean, I guess it doesn't really matter. I know I'm in enough trouble already with what happened, so I suppose it doesn't make much difference which way you write it down, unless you think that I won't be able to serve my sentence for "shopping" at the same time as my other sentences, in which case I'd ask that you erase this part, and just put down instead: "Kenny Broadhead, he took the Fifth when it came to the 'shopping' parts."

That's the amendment of the American Constitution, by the way, that I'm talking about there. Not "taking the Fifth" like, "Kenny stole a bottle of Jack Daniels," or something. We didn't shop for liquor the way we shopped for guitars.

All right, all right, now we're gettin' to the shopping. So it's like this: Every year, me and Delmas and Wardrow get in our truck the day after Labor Day weekend to go do our shopping for . . . Oh, man! Wait! I have to tell you one other thing first! It's about where Cokesbury is, in relationship to the things that are all around it.

We're out in the country a bit, sure, but we're pretty close to all of the big cities here in the central part of North Carolina, and every one of those big cities has a big college or two in it.

So, let's see, within an hour or so or Cokesbury there's the University of North Carolina Albemarle, and North Carolina NASCAR Mechanics' College, and Cary-Yankee University, and Marlboro-Camel Tech, and Duke University (that's not named after that skinny black fella that Missus Pepper Prong hates, by the way, it's named after the mayonnaise company), and East Carolina Barbecue Academy, and Fuquay-Varina Gynecology Institute, and all sorts of other colleges, all over the place.

Other than hams and cigarettes, in fact, colleges are North Carolina's biggest business, or so I'm told. Hard to imagine so many kids would want to go to school for more than seven years, but I guess that's just the world we live in these days.

Now, living around all of these colleges for so long, here's what me and Delmas and Wardrow figured out through our careful powers of observation: Wherever there's colleges, there's college students. And then we figured out that wherever there's college students, some of them are college boys. And then, after that, we figured out that wherever there's college boys, there's college girls that those college boys want to impress and court. Except at Wade-Badin Bible College, anyway. They don't allow coveting there.

OK, so here's the best part we figured out, the cleverest bit, again using our careful powers of observation: What's one of the ways that lots of college boys try to impress college girls? Why, by playing guitars and other instruments loudly out the windows of their dorm rooms, of course!

I mean, you know how a bullfrog's got its croak, right? And a tom turkey has got its gobble? And that makes 'em irresistible to the cowfrogs and the hen turkeys? Well, sir, for college girls in these parts, a boy with an amped-up Gibson SG or Fender Stratocaster guitar playing "Free Bird" or "Flirtin' with Disaster" or "Sweet Home Alabama" or "Jim Dandy" or "Jessica" or what have you out of his college dorm room window is just as irresistible as that bullfrog or tom turkey will ever be to their fairer counterparts. Maybe even more so.

So now that you understand that part, here's the thing about "shopping" and how that fits into the story. What me and Wardrow and Delmas do is this: We drive slowly around a couple of these colleges at the start of each new school year, and we listen for the six-string cries of those courtin' college boys, playing with their windows open since it's warm here in early September, and so all the college girls around can hear them louder that way, the better to be drawn to their virtuoso guitar skills, like flies to a spider's web. Except that the college boys aren't generally planning to kill the college girls, or at least not most of the time. But we'll get to that part of the story later, I guess.

Anyway, back to the shopping. So as the three of us drive around these colleges, we write down the locations of all the lonely guitar boys that are playing their mating calls out of first-floor windows. And this is because we have observed that when they leave their rooms, most of them will lock their doors, but they won't close their windows, and nine times out of ten, they'll just leave their guitars laying on their beds or propped up against their desks, or right under their windows, even, still plugged into their amps, so that they can start the courtin' again as soon as they get back to their rooms.

So come dusk, when the college boys head to the race car track or the library or wherever it is they go in the evening, we put on our best Sunday-go-to-meeting clothes, and we amble around the colleges, making our way back to those first-floor rooms with guitars, checking to see if they're occupied. More often than not, the lights are on, we can see everything clearly, and it's a simple job to reach through the window, grab the ax, and saunter back to the truck, like we were just visiting music professors or something.

We can usually get maybe half a dozen six-string guitars a year, and maybe a bass guitar every other year or so. We keep the best ones for the band, and we usually sell the leftover ones to other bands we know, or pawn 'em down in Fayetteville by the army base, since those soldiers down there just love them some pawn shop guitars, let me tell you. Every five years or so, we'll use some of the money we make to buy Wardrow some new drums, since it's harder to get a drum kit out of a dorm room window than it is to lift a guitar. We learned that lesson the hard way one year, when Wardrow slipped while climbing out a window and punctured his bowel when he fell on a high-hat stand.

The best part of our system, I have to say, is that with so many colleges around here, we can rotate them year by year, so we don't hit the same ones more than once every four years, when the kids we shopped from last time will have graduated, and a new crop of courtin' college boys will have arrived. Easy pickin's!

So how's that for putting the old powers of observation to good purpose? It makes me feel smart to know that nobody else seems to have figured this kind of thing out the way that

Delmas and Wardrow and me did. It's kind of a nice little side business for us all, sort of a third job, as it were, after the Doornail Dead De-bugging Depot and the Burzürkers. Seasonal work, you might say.

What's that? Well, yeah, I do suppose it's wrong, on some plane, sure. But the way I see it, these kids didn't buy the guitars in the first place most of the time but got 'em from their parents instead. This is why they hardly ever file police reports, since they know they were idiots for losing stuff that their mamas and daddies bought for 'em, and they don't want to make a stink about it accordingly. It's an important lesson we teach these kids: Hey! lock your stuff up, you dumb guitar boys, because now the smart guitar boys who did close and latch their windows are the ones who are gonna get the girls, while you study alone, right?

I do want to be clear that we never break anything, we never force anything, and sometimes we can get the guitars out without even getting much more than an arm though the open window of the dorm room. So, you know, that barely qualifies as stealing, the way I see it, any more than it would count as stealing if one of those college boys left his guitar out in the middle of a field unattended, and I happened to come along and find it there. Or if he put it down in the back of my truck to rest his arm, and I happened to drive away while it was there. I just sort of see it as a finders-keepers thing, you know? Except that we just improve our odds of finding things by making our shopping trips beforehand, that's all. That doesn't seem like a crime to me, but, uh, you do remember that part I said earlier about "taking the Fifth," right? I mean, if this stuff's gonna get me in more trouble, then I'd rather you just tear it out of your notebooks or erase it from your tapes there, OK?

But, you know, I just couldn't really get to the beginning of the story you want me to tell and have it make any sense to you unless you understood these parts of it first, so if you do erase the part about shopping from your notebooks or the tape, just try to keep it in your brains, so that everything else I tell you makes sense later, even if I didn't say it officially, since I took the Fifth and everything. Can you do that? Great! Thanks!

OK, then, so now you know about me, and you know about Cokesbury, and you know about the Burzürkers, and you know about the "shopping." Plus you know about Missus Pepper Prong, but you don't need to know about her, like I said before.

And I think that's all you need to know by way of background explanation, so now I think I can get to the start of this story finally.

Here's what happened.

Me and Delmas and Wardrow went shopping at Marlboro-Camel Tech at the start of school time this year. We hadn't been there for a while, since those boys tend to like bongs and guns and race cars more than they like guitars, but it's worth a visit every now and again, since the ones that do play guitars tend to like things like Gibson Flying V's and Explorers and such like. Real metal guitars. Nothing sissy about the Marlboro-Camel guitar boys.

We had a good and quick afternoon of being observant, and we picked out five nice guitars in five first-floor rooms, then went over to the Efland Road House for a couple of hours to catch the early-bird stripper special. They do a nice spread there, good buffet, lots of meat, three different sauces, and they put the prettiest girls on the pole for happy hour, so it's a good place to go when you don't have other places to be. We had a good dinner and got a good show. Wholesome, like. Nothing too nasty, understand?

So then we headed back over to Marlboro-Camel Tech and we sauntered around all cool and casual like and were able to get four of the five guitars with no muss and no fuss, just grab and go, toss 'em under the tarp in the back of the truck and move on out. The fifth guitar wasn't in the room where we spotted it. Kid who lived there must have had a gig that night, maybe. Or somebody else was shopping and got there before us. I can't help but think that someone else must have figured out our system by now. It ain't rocket science, after all.

And then we loaded up and got ready to head back to Cokesbury when Delmas just happened to turn his head in the right direction at the right time and this whole story really gets started. You know how it ends, I guess, but since you want this for your notes and your tape then I guess you want me to tell you what he saw, right? Right, thought so.

Here's what it was: Delmas noticed a Dumpster in an alley behind one of those dorms, and that tends to capture his attention because, well, you know, you can find all sorts of great things in Dumpsters. Televisions. Computers. Porno magazines. Sometimes even a sofa. One time, we found a go-cart. And another time, we found a refrigerator that still had beer in it! Those kids, man, they just don't know how to take care of their stuff. It's a shame, really. If only their parents knew!

What? Oh, yeah, this time. Well, what Delmas saw this time was a big bull fiddle sticking out of the Dumpster. Well, not the bull fiddle itself, actually, but a bull fiddle case. A hard one, not one of them cheap cloth ones. You know the difference? Cloth cases are worthless, they just get wet in the rain or when you spill your beer on them, and then your instrument gets wet, and you can't tune it, and the strings get rusty and cut your fingers, and it's just a mess all around.

So this was a big bull fiddle case, and when you see a big bull fiddle case, then there's probably a bull fiddle inside it, right? That's what we figured, anyway. We had bass guitars aplenty, sure, but we'd never had one of those big, stand-up bull fiddles with a bow before, so Delmas let out a shout and we stopped quick like and backed up a bit and then pulled the truck into alley behind the dorm, right up against the Dumpster to see what was what. A bull fiddle could be a nice change of pace for a scum rock band like the Burzürkers, you know? Delmas could do some jazzy stuff with that, or he could just slap at it and spin it all cool like during Wardrow's drum solo. The possibilities were endless.

Now, since we hadn't ever had a bull fiddle before, no one thought much of anything when Delmas went to pull it out of the Dumpster and it was a whole lot heavier than he thought it was going to be, so he was really struggling with the thing. I generally don't like to get out of the drivers' seat once the engine's running, in case I got to beat a hasty getaway, so when I saw Delmas trying to wrestle that big old bull fiddle, I pushed Wardrow and told him to get out and lend a hand. With a bit more struggling, the two of them managed to get the case to the truck, slid it in the bed with the other guitars, pulled the tarp over the pile and then, zoom bang, we was on our way back to the barn on my back pasture, which is where we keep all our new band equipment until we decide what we want to keep and what we want to sell, and where we also do our rehearsing, since it's remote and quiet-like out there.

Our curiosity was itching at us like a chigger infestation the whole way back, and after we got the regular guitars and that heavy old bull fiddle case into the barn, we decided that we'd start our investigations and evaluations with that unexpected Dumpster surprise first thing. The hard case had a lock on it, and the lock was locked, but that ain't nothin' but a thing when it comes to instrument cases like that. You barely need any tools to crack those things, just stick a file under the hasp, wiggle the halves of the case a bit with a little bit of pressure against the little springy hinge thing, and they usually pop really easy. Don't know why they bother to put them on those cases at all the first place. It ain't like thieves are gonna look at a guitar case and say, "Whoa, no way, not gonna steal that one, it's locked up tight-like!" Just a silly waste of time and materials, if you ask me.

What? Well, I'm getting there. I'm just trying to let you know what we were thinking. There wasn't any malice or bad thoughts in any of this stuff, you know? We didn't mean the guitar boys any harm, and we only took their instruments so that we could bring joy and happiness to all the scum rock fans in these parts. It means so much to them, you know? And imagine how they'd feel when we showed up with bull fiddle, like something you'd see at a fancy show in the city. Damn! The possibilities!

So, well, once again, you know how this part goes, I guess, but just for the record, we popped open that cheap little lock, and then we opened up the other little clasps that don't have locks on them — there was four, if you need to know that — and then we flipped open the top of the case and, well, you sure can imagine how surprised we were that instead of a big bull fiddle inside that case, there was a girl instead. Real surprised is how surprised, if you can't guess that. Even more surprised than the time we found a solid half-pound of hash in the little case where you keep picks in one guitar case, or the time that another case didn't have any guitar in it at all, just a mess of fireworks. Good ones! From China!

So we were even more surprised than that in this case, even before we really looked at what we were looking at. Because . . . well, this is a little delicate, I have to say, so I have to think about my words here. Hmmm. You know what a bull fiddle's shaped like, right? OK, well, that's not really the same shape as a girl, so, ummm, whoever had put her in there had had to make some, uh, adjustments to her, I guess you'd say. Some parts weren't where they normally were on a girl. And other things weren't all connected, you know? But she did all fit in there, I have to say. That was surprising in and of itself. Oh, did I tell you that she was dead? Yessir, she was. She was dead in that there bull fiddle case.

So we were quite surprised, as you sure can imagine. Did I say that already? Well, that's how surprised we were, enough that I should say it twice. There was a lot of surprise between the three of us, and I'd be lying if I didn't admit that there was some cussing and exclaiming from us all when we got that biggest of big surprises.

I was the one who closed the case back up, and I hitched back those four latches that didn't have locks on them. I couldn't latch back the one with the lock on it, since it was broken. Useless things, those locks, like I said. Half the time, they get broke on their own, you know? Even when you're not trying to force them. Don't know why they bother.

But anyway, back to the story, there the three of us were in the barn with a bull fiddle case filled with a real big surprise. Or four of us, I guess, if you count the girl. I suspect she was surprised to find herself in a bull fiddle case too. We sat for a spell and made all the sorts of sounds you make when you're surprised, like "Whoa, man!" and "Jeezum crow!" and "Who'da thunk?" and "Tarnation!" and such like, and then we got quiet, the way we all do when we start thinking hard about things.

And then we started to discuss what we might do at that point, faced with such a first-class, world-record surprise. Wardrow suggested we just load the bull fiddle case up and take it back to the Dumpster, but then Delmas smartly said that if someone saw us drop it off, then they'd for sure think we were the scoundrels who put that girl in the case in the first place, and that just wouldn't do, since rearranging a girl to make her fit in a bull fiddle case was a whole different level of offense than shopping for guitars, and we just weren't that type of criminals.

So I suggested that maybe we should just call the police and tell them what we had found, but then Wardrow smartly suggested that it would be hard to explain how that bull fiddle case ended up in my barn without explaining what we were doing there at Marlboro-Camel Tech. It just didn't seem like a good idea to us all to have to explain the whole "shopping" thing to the authorities when we were just trying to figure out how to be good citizens and do the right thing. I mean, yes, I explained the "shopping" thing to you just now, but once an arrest has already happened, that kind of changes things. We didn't have an arrest yet that night, so that sort of changes the way I think about the whole thing, now.

There were some other ideas, but every time someone said one, someone else smartly said why it wouldn't work. So we just sort of circled round and round the problem, until we backed into the idea that the best thing we could do was to destroy the evidence, as it was, and get back to our normal routines and pretend like the thing just didn't happen. We hadn't done that girl any harm. We hadn't put her in the bull fiddle case. And we didn't even get that old case shopping but just picked it out of the Dumpster. No crime there, anywhere along the way.

Well, that's what we thought then anyway. I understand now that y'all consider handling a body like that to be a crime, but we didn't know that then, did we?

So, let's see, what was next? Well, we argued a bit about the best way to do the evidence disposal, looking at the good points and the bad points on all the options. Burying was a lot of work, and you never know when some bad animal might go digging things up. You could toss something heavy like that bull fiddle in a pond, as another idea, but you'd need a boat to get out deep enough to make that work, and we weren't really sure about whether the plastic bull fiddle case would float or not. It seemed like a lot of work to make that option happen, only to have it come bobbing up a week later or so.

And that's how we eventually decided that the best thing we could do was to burn the evidence. It seemed respectful when we thought about it. We didn't know what had happened to that girl so that she ended up in the bull fiddle case, but if we burned the case with her in it, then that would destroy the evidence, and it wouldn't be much worse than a cremation, if you think about it. We'd stand around respectful-like, have a moment of silence, take off our ball caps, and treat the whole thing like a proper funeral. We knew she'd have liked it better if people she knew were there, but we weren't about to go making inquiries, you understand.

We dragged the bull fiddle case out to my burn barrel, but you know what? The bottom of a bull fiddle won't fit inside a burn barrel, even a big fifty-five-gallon one like we had. It's not the height that's the problem: you can put tall stuff in the barrel and light the bottom, and then stuff it down into the barrel as it burns up. No sir, the problem was the width: the bottom of that bull fiddle just wouldn't go into the barrel, and when we put it in upside-down, well, then that sort of got us to thinking that as it burned and we had to stuff the case down into the can, we might have to touch and see some things that we just didn't think would be respectful.

So we found a spot over on the side of the barn, shielded from the road, and we cleared the weeds away, and we dug a little bit like you would for a barbecue, except it was shaped like a bull fiddle case and not a pig, and we put that big plastic hard case into the pit, and then Wardrow went to the truck and got a jug of gasoline, and we poured it all over the case and into the pit, and then I got a box of matches from the barn, the wooden kind that you can light in the rain, and I lit one on the first try, and I tossed it into the pit.

It went up right quick and loud-like, with a "whump!" sound, and we all got a bit singed from standing too close to the pit. We backed off, and after we patted down our clothes to make sure we weren't smoldering and checked to see that our beards and eyebrows were okay, then we stood back a bit to do the respectful part, thinking things would just burn up quick, and then we'd rake the ground and get on with forgetting about what happened.

But it didn't turn out to be that easy. Once the gas burned up, well, the case didn't really seem like it wanted to burn. We splashed some more gas on it and tossed another couple few matches from a safer distance. It took more matches this time, since it's harder to throw 'em and keep 'em lit if you're not right up on the pit, you know? But the same thing happened again, and the fire sort of smoldered out, with the bull fiddle case looking a bit scorched but not really burnt, if you know what I mean.

So we decided to make a more traditional fire, and we got some wood from the barn and some old, damp logs from the edge of the woods and some kindling from the scrap pile, and then we lit it more like you would a campfire. Delmas got in close to put the match in and to sort of blow it like you do, but there must have been some gas fumes still in there, and he got singed again when another unexpected "whump!" jumped out of the pit. This time, it did take his eyebrows off. He was pretty funny-looking and mad, but we reminded him that we needed to be respectful, and he settled down a bit, understanding that this was just one of those days when you had to take the cards that were dealt to you.

Eventually, the fire got going pretty good, so we were thinking that our plan was going to work out after all. The plastic bull fiddle case started to smoke, and then some flames popped out on some parts of it, and then eventually it caught fire good, and it started to burn even better than the logs did.

Except, you know how when logs burn, they eventually sort of start to get hotter and smaller and then fall apart into little pieces, and then just ashes and cinder? Well, that's not quite what happened to the bull fiddle case.

I guess if I had to describe it, I would say that what it did was more like what happens when you put a Styrofoam cup into a fire. Have you ever seen that? It's kinda cool, actually: It sort of bubbles and bubbles and bubbles and crinkles and folds up a bit, but it just keeps bubbling and burning for a long, long time, and when it's done, it's not really like ashes that are left, but more like a little blob of some kind. If you poke a stick in it, it'll cling to the stick, and you can sort of model it like clay or something, and when it cools, it stays in the same shape it was when it finished burning.

So that's what that bull fiddle case did, if you can imagine that. It bubbled and bubbled and bubbled, and sort of crinkled and crumpled and got smaller and smaller, but, well, it's kind of hard to say this part, but as it got more bubbly and smaller, you could start to see what was inside it taking shape, and it wasn't a bull fiddle in there. So first you could start to see a leg here. And then an arm there. Maybe a foot. A head, later. And the plastic just got smaller and tighter around it all, and then you could really sort of see the things that whoever had put the girl into the bull fiddle case needed to do to get her in there, and, well, sir, I have to tell you, it was a little bit disturbing to us all. It was hard for us to hold our respectful postures at that point, if I'm honest with you. But we did our best.

And the whole thing just kept bubbling and getting smaller and smaller and more like shrink wrap now, if you can imagine that. Black shrink wrap, anyway. You couldn't see through it, actually, but you could see what was wrapped up in it. We talked about whether we should poke it with sticks like you would with a Styrofoam cup, but that didn't seem respectful either, so we just added some more wood to the pit, and that got stuck in the black plastic too, all of it just sort of melting and bubbling together like a big black pile of tar or something, except with parts sticking out it that weren't logs, if you get my drift.

That was about all the three of us could take, I have to say, even though we're all fellows with strong constitutions who have seen some things, let me tell you. We were still trying to be respectful and do the right thing, but at some point I suggested that maybe the best way we could be respectful was to not actually watch what was happening but instead just go into the barn, and then let the fire do what it was going to do and hope for the best come morning when it had all run its course and cooled off.

So that's what we did. We sorted the guitars. We had some beers. We talked about this, and we talked about that, and we tried to not think about what was happening out there. Occasionally one of us would peek out just to make sure the fire wasn't spreading, since safety's important, even when you're dealing with a big surprise situation like this. And then we drank some more beers, and we got quiet, and we got out the sleeping bags and the cots that we kept there for late-night rehearsals, and we all bedded down with our thoughts and a couple more beers and waited to see what the morning would bring.

I was the first one up, like I usually am, since I'm the one who usually has to get everyone moving when we've got a full day of work with the Doornail Dead De-bugging Depot, and I pulled my coat on and walked out to the fire pit we'd made. It was done burning and cold, but there in the middle of it was a hard piece of black plastic shrink wrap that showed you everything inside it, including some parts we hadn't been able to see the night before. There was less to them than there probably should have been, bones mainly, I guess, but those shapes are kinda hard to miss, and we knew we had a problem on our hands now, since after all we'd done, we were still going to have to do some digging and burying or boating and sinking or hauling and dumping or something.

We had shovels in the shed and no boat, so it didn't take much conversation for us to decide that burying was the best course of action. We were hopeful that the black shrink wrap would keep smells inside and discourage any critters from digging up our work, so there was at least that benefit from all the burns and things we'd experienced from the fire the night before.

And, well, that's what we were up to when y'all rolled up with sirens blazing and guns drawn. I'd guess the hole we'd dug was about three feet deep, based on where it came up to me, but we hadn't gotten to the point of moving the big black plastic blob into it. You know the story from that point, I guess: We laid down on the ground all quiet and peaceful-like as you asked, and we pointed out the spot where the bull fiddle case was, and that young fella threw up on his uniform, and you cuffed us and brought us here, and that's where we are now.

Who'da thunk that Marlboro-Camel Tech would have had a security camera in that alley where the Dumpster was, and who'da thunk that we'd have parked right in front of it so you could ID my truck? What were they trying to protect there? The trash? Seems strange, when nobody ever nabbed us on surveillance before. Just one of those things, I suppose. I appreciate you telling me about it. I suppose you learn something new every day. I'll keep that in mind.

Same thing about that boy who killed the girl and put her in the case. Gosh, if I'd done something like that, then I sure wouldn't have gotten drunk that very night and told my buddies about it. Some folks just can't hold their liquor, can they? I guess he was right surprised when his friends called you and then he led you fellas there but the bull fiddle case was gone. We'd have done his dirty work for him, if he'd been smarter and quieter. Boy like that's got no business in college, does he? What's the point?

What's that? Remorse? Well, sure, of course I feel some remorse. Nobody deserves to be put into a bull fiddle case that way. Last night when I was in the solitary cell, I got to thinking about who that girl was and what her family and her friends might have thought had they known what was happening to her. I'm not sure you can ever get over something like that. It's a dirty shame, all around. That boy messed up a whole lot of lives, me and Wardrow's and Delmas' included. I hope you throw the book at him. He sure deserves it.

Some people just got no sense, y'know?

ACKNOWLEDGMENTS

I landed my first paid freelance writing gig at the age of 13, hired to be the teen columnist and editor for the base newspaper at Mitchel Field, on New York's Long Island. I also completed my first substantial short story around that time, a work of historical fiction about Lady Jane Grey, then won a statewide poetry contest organized by a major newspaper in Rhode Island a year or so later. That poetry contest was sponsored by one of Newport's larger fraternal lodges, and I was given the opportunity to read for its members, all of them adults, who seemed to like what I presented to them. I deeply wish that I still had those works today, and I regret that I do not remember the names of the teachers and publishers and community members who so encouraged me in those early creative pursuits. Whoever they were, I still appreciate them, as it was their early affirmation that led me to actively focusing on writing whatever I could, whenever I could, for whatever outlets would have me. And when there were no outlets, I kept writing anyway. The act of scribbling became an existential one for me — a habit, a passion, an obsession, and a love — which linked and underpinned everything I ever did professionally over the ensuing decades.

The stories in this collection were originally written as acts of self-entertainment, procrastination, and/or the compulsive scribbling tendencies noted above, while I was otherwise engaged in writing for various employers, freelance clients, and nonprofit boards. The oldest stories were finished in the mid-1990s, while the most recent came to life in the late-2010s. As my creative process has always involved lots of research, lots of pondering, lots of shuffling around the house muttering to myself, mad bursts of frantic typing, inevitably followed by more shuffling and muttering, my first expressions of gratitude directly related to this book must go to my wife, Marcia, and my daughter, Katelin, who humored me along the way, with love, and who were always excited whenever stories finally cohered to the points where they could read them.

While I did not share these stories with them in real time, my parents (Colonel Charles R. Smith, Jr., USMC, and Linda Ann Waters Smith), my sister (E. Paige Smith Duft), my brother-in-law (Dana Duft), and my son-in-law (John Cross) have also been enthusiastic supporters of my professional and creative work, for which I am grateful. I look forward to them being able to finally read what I have been working on stealthily and steadily for so many years, except in the case of my father, who is no longer with us. Earlier in my life, one of my grandmothers (Cora Mae Hege Smith) and one of my aunts (Patti Waters Teter) offered particularly strong influences on my developing creative aesthetic by introducing me to a wide variety of books and art and music that I might never have tumbled across otherwise on my own. Thanks to them too.

Around 2016, I was culling files and cleaning folders on various hard drives after a computer crash, and I placed all these stories, written in many different places and times, in one digital space for the first time ever. Finally realizing that there was enough material to constitute a legitimately hefty collection, possibly of interest beyond my immediate family circle, I mashed the stories together and sent them off to my friend Keith Ammann, who had been one of my editors when I wrote for *Metroland* in Albany, New York in the 1990s. Keith was the first person to read *Ubulembu and Other Stories* as a single body of work, and as an artisan of red ink, he added immense value to the text, through both pure, hard copy-editing, and also through valuable suggestions on order, flow, and cuts to the original manuscript. Brilliant work, Keith, thank you!

Fortified with a well-edited manuscript, I slowly and selectively began shopping the story collection, before getting professionally distracted (as one does) by another wonderful project: writing *Side by Side in Eternity: The Lives Behind Adjacent American Military Graves* (McFarland Books, Jefferson, North Carolina, 2023), with my U.S. Naval Academy and Naval Supply Corps School classmate, Rear Admiral James McNeal, SC, USN (Ret.). Jim and I enjoyed that project so much that we are already pushing forward with another, provisionally titled *Crucibles: History's Most Formidable Rites of Passage*, this time ably represented by Mark Gottlieb of Trident Media Group. We're expecting that to be published in 2025, fingers crossed. It has been a delight to reconnect and work with Jim on these projects. He's a fine writing partner. Other life-long Naval Academy friends, most notably Jamie Jaquet, Greg Partney, Adam Paterson, Tom Kolongowski, and Allen Walther, have also encouraged and supported me and my work in ways that they may or may not have realized over the years, but for which I am grateful nonetheless.

The other greatest sources of support and inspiration in my creative life have arisen from my status as a deeply seasoned internet warrior, having been an active member of various online communities since the early 1990s, and having launched my own website in 1995, about as early as it was possible for private individuals to do so. My first significant online creative community was the Xnet2 Collective, featuring the late Wilson Smith, the late Lynne Austin, Imelda "Mellie" Eggleston, Cathy Ross, Evan "Funk" Davies, Paul Terrell, Glenn Susser, Rebecca Kerewsky, Robert "Goat" Beveridge, Bob Farace, and others. Later came the scabrous creative horror shows of Upstate Wasted and Upstate Ether, where Stephen Gaylord, Keith Sonin, Gaven Richards, Matt Heuston, John Rodat, the late Shawn Stone, and countless others, usually anonymously or pseudonymously, team-wrote some of the most addictively entertaining, disturbingly hilarious, and often just plain wrong material ever to clog the internet's pipes. I truly believe that I produced some of my finest written storytelling on those platforms, never under my own name, the vast majority of that material now dissipated through digital entropy. I consider it my creative sand mandala: time-consuming to construct, beautiful in its moment, then liberating to destroy.

Over the past 15 years or so, my primary online community has been the Fall Online Forum (FOF), where Dannyno, Divvey, Bzfgt, Delmore, Pott, Dead Seminal, Academic Hamilton, Rainmaster, Buy Kurious, Snowy, Aubrey the Cat, The Hip Priestess, Mr. Marshall, Elvis Chomsky (RIP), Starsky-Tandoori, DJ Ash, A Worried Man,

Chris Shaw, Steve in Leighton, Jim Kidder, Hiccup Percy, Dr John Rock, Neal Cassady, Osmooms, Beck's Knob, Grumpy Northern Git, Spiring, and many others have amused, educated, entertained, argued with and inspired me in various evolving ways. I do know most of their real names, but in keeping with FOF convention, I shall respectfully not divulge them here. I will, however, call one Forum member out by his full name, since it's already in the public domain: Steve Pringle, author of *You Must Get Them All: The Fall on Record* (Route Publishing, 2022), the best book yet written about one of the most fascinating musical groups of the post-punk era. I remain pleased to have been involved with Steve on the periphery of that project in its nascent days, and commend his work to your attention.

I must also extend a fond and awed expression of gratitude to the amazing Rick Harris of Fillmore South and Little Aleppo, tragically struck down by cancer in April 2021, way too young to go. Better known by his strenuously-maintained online byline, Thoughts on the Dead, Rick was the most gifted story-teller I have personally encountered in recent decades, and maybe ever. In 2017, I described his novel, *A Book With No Title*, as the 21st Century's Greatest Work of Fiction, and nothing has happened since then to dissuade me of that notion. Rick also built a truly beautiful online community during his brief, prolific moment in the creative sun, and it was a thrill and an honor and a hoot to have been a small part of his gloriously deranged semi-fictional world.

My own long-running website (jericsmith.com) has also had a faithful cohort of regular readers, while several other websites, writers, and artists have become closely cross-linked to my platforms through shared readership and mutual support over the decades. I am grateful for and appreciative of them all, with Jeff Claus, Greg Goth, Roger Owen Green, Chuck Miller, Carl Johnson, Rob Madeo, Rob Heinsoo, Jed Davis, and Buggy Jive (Bryan Thomas) earning special thanks and affection. I also must thank Jed and Buggy for making music that consistently moved me throughout the years in which these stories marinated. I have been proud to write regularly about their amazing songs, shows, and recordings, always delighted by any opportunity that arises for me to use my own online, print, or television platforms to share their brilliance with others.

Finally, I must extend my heartfelt thanks and appreciation to Jen Knox, Chris Shanahan and their team at Unleash Creatives/Unleash Lit, along with Richard C. McPherson, final judge of the Unleash Creatives 2023 Book Prize, awarded to *Ubulembu and Other Stories*. While I am proud of all my professional writing, these stories are the most dear to me, on some plane. They are not reporting, or reviewing, or researching, or describing existing narratives or events, but are instead tales spun in whole from within me, which only exist because I imagined them, and that feels different, somehow. I was most impressed by Unleash Creatives' platform, editorial approach, and holistic community-building interests when I first submitted this book for their consideration in August 2022, and I am most proud to have my work now made available to you via their fine imprint.

Thank you, thank you, thank you! You all move and inspire me, and I am truly grateful.

ABOUT THE AUTHOR

J. Eric Smith is a native of South Carolina's Low Country who lived and worked in 13 different states before settling happily with his wife, Marcia, in Northern Arizona's Red Rocks Region, where he now hikes and climbs more things than he probably should. Smith is a graduate of the United States Naval Academy, the Naval Supply Corps School, and the University at Albany's Rockefeller College of Public Affairs and Policy. After serving for eleven years with the U.S. Naval Nuclear Propulsion Program, he transitioned to the civilian sector, working as a fundraising professional, communications director, operations manager, and four-time nonprofit executive director, while also managing numerous contract, consulting, and board roles. Throughout his charitable and government careers, Smith continued to work as a writer, earning more bylines that he could possibly remember for a variety of alternative newsweeklies, trade journals, nonprofit periodicals, magazines, and newspapers. He was also a digital space pioneer, launching the first version of his long-running website in 1995. A large archive of his articles remains available at jericsmith.com, along with new writing on a wide variety of topics.